'Now for the reality,' he cut in harshly. 'When the ship blew up last night we were the lucky ones...' She realised now that his face was sombre with signs of an immense strain. That fact, even more than his words, made her flesh begin to creep. It prepared her in some way for what he told her next.

'When I fished you out of the water,' he went on, 'you were tangled up among some wreckage, otherwise you'd have drowned, because, as you've guessed, you were knocked unconscious. We were swept away from the ship...' He seemed to consider his words for a moment and then he said, 'We beached here through sheer good luck. Or did we?' He examined her expression. 'How much can you take?'

'How—what do you mean?' she asked, cold fear stilling her thoughts.

'We're alone. On a rock atoll. We don't know whether there's fresh water or not. Or where we are, whether on the main shipping routes or somewhere...' he smiled wryly '...less frequented.'

Books you will enjoy
by SALLY HEYWOOD

STEPS TO HEAVEN

For Rachel, sacrifice and dedication would have
to go hand in hand if she was to turn her dream
of being a successful singer into reality. Though
Elliot Priest might have been another dream
come true, he threatened her secret ambition, so
she knew what she must do. But would success
really be so sweet if she couldn't have Elliot?

CASTLE OF DESIRE

If he knew the truth Marc Vila might reconsider
the assumptions he'd made about her, but
Sarella couldn't take that risk. She'd made a
promise based on friendship to pretend to be his
younger brother's fiancée, and, anyway, there
was another reason why she just mustn't let
Marc get any closer—she found the ex-racing-
driver incredibly attractive...

LOVE ISLAND

BY

SALLY HEYWOOD

MILLS & BOON LIMITED
ETON HOUSE   18-24 PARADISE ROAD
RICHMOND   SURREY   TW9 1SR

*First published in Great Britain 1992
by Mills & Boon Limited*

© Sally Heywood 1992

*Australian copyright 1992
Philippine copyright 1992
This edition 1992*

ISBN 0 263 77511 9

*Set in Times Roman 11 on 12 pt.
01-9204-51383 C*

Made and printed in Great Britain

CHAPTER ONE

THERE was something rough underneath her left cheek. Judi turned her head and rested the other side of her face against whatever she was lying on. Despite her discomfort she felt too drowsy to move, let alone open her eyes to find out where she was. Maybe she was at home? she thought dreamily. But no. There was something with the texture of sand beneath her. She could feel it, rough yet yielding, against her thighs and breasts. It was almost as if she were naked. She let her fingers claw gently into the grainy warmth. Yes, it had to be sand. Hot sand. It felt wonderful.

The surprising fact that she must be lying on a beach didn't arouse any other questions for some time. She felt too warm, too comfortable to want to think, to move. And something soft and firm was making its way over her scalp, moving through her hair, over her head and slowly back down her neck again. She smiled in her dreams. Whatever it was moved on down her spine, checking and caressing with a sure touch. She came to with a start. What was happening? She tried to turn her head, but a sudden pain shot through her body and she gave an involuntary gasp.

'Keep still,' commanded a voice like black velvet from somewhere above her.

With a push of energy she forced her eyes open. A blaze of silver made her wince, shutting them tight, then she tried again, opening them more cautiously, squinting through her long black lashes until she could make out the surprising fact that she really was lying on a stretch of sand just as she had imagined. Close to her eyes, each separate grain glinted with all the colours of the spectrum, but the overall dazzle was pure silver. It hurt. She closed her eyes and let the throb of pain recede.

'Take your time,' murmured the voice again. It was a warm voice, a rich, masculine caress, so close that it was like someone speaking inside her head, until she realised it couldn't be so, it was too real, and then she felt herself drift away and the voice and the bright blaze of silver faded to the edge of consciousness again.

Next time she became aware of her surroundings she already knew she was lying on a beach, and in the distance came the rhythmic hiss of the surf to confirm it. At almost the same moment memory came racing back with a sickening rush. Unable to stop herself, Judi jerked upright, gasping aloud as she did so, unexpected arrows of pain lacerating her body. Her breath gouged in and out, but in the midst of it all came something else. It was a gentle touch over her bare skin, soothing the tension. As she felt it pressuring the pain away, reassuring her that someone—but who?—was taking care of her, she made an effort to roll over on to her back. Then she looked up.

Against the glare of the tropical sun she could only see a silhouette. It rose massively, protectingly above her, and when she focused properly it took on definition, a rugged shape, all male, burnished muscle and broad shoulders, a face full of concern peering down into her own. The shadows are part of his hair, she thought. Midnight black, touchable. Then the sun lit his face as he moved back to assess her reactions, light blazing from brow to jaw, revealing a tough, strong-boned face, bold features, a ruthlessness in the jagged line of cheekbone and jaw and the reckless mouth. Shock waves coursed through her. He was a stranger. And what she had taken for concern was no longer there. What remained sent shudders through her. He was too hard, too strong, too powerful. He could annihilate her.

Her limbs fluttered in what she told herself was an irrational fear as she remembered his intimate touch as she had faded in and out of consciousness, but just now, when he had caressed her, making the pain go, something like tenderness had been there. He had taken care of her. Her spasm of fear passed. Somehow she knew she was safe.

Dark lashes flickered on her cheeks as she struggled out of oblivion, and she forced open her lavender-blue eyes and smiled trustingly up at him.

His response was difficult to gauge now he had his back to the sun.

She tried to raise her head so that she could see him properly. With the sand biting into her back as it had bitten into her breasts and stomach when she lay face down before, she squirmed to get up, jerking fully awake. Then her glance alighted on her slim brown body lying full length on the pale sand. And what she saw swept her with a blush of embarrassment—she was nearly nude!

Her hands flew to her breasts. What had happened to her clothes? There was a scrap of scarlet tied round her hips. It just covered her thighs. A surge of self-consciousness made her flick an alarmed glance at the stranger bending over her. Eyes as bright and blue as the Pacific were watching her reactions with pinpoint interest.

With a flurry she tugged at the scrap of filmy material, but she could tell it was only enough to cover a small part of her anatomy. Then suddenly the memories started to flood back.

In a panic she tried to scramble to her knees, but the stranger placed his hands on her shoulders and firmly forced her back on to the sand. Her eyes opened wide in renewed alarm, but his touch was decisive.

'Steady,' he told her in his dark voice. 'There's no hurry. You're not going anywhere. Take it easy——'

She allowed him to hold her still for a moment, quivering as his blue eyes lazed over her naked form. If she struggled to get away he was stronger than she was and... She felt trapped, nerves taut, waiting for what might happen next. There were a million questions shrieking inside her head now as she was coming round, but, irrationally, the one that sprang to mind concerned her hair. That expensive bob! What did it look like? His expression mirrored nothing back. 'My hair...!' she croaked, finding it strange that her voice refused to obey her. She gave a hysterical giggle as the sight and sound of the catastrophe bore in on her again. It had been a nightmare of noise and screams and...

'Steady,' he murmured, 'steady!' He took her in his arms and cradled her head in the crook, stroking her hair, smoothing it just the way it was meant to go. She wanted to blurt, Where am I? but stopped herself in time. Her rescuer or whoever he was—and despite the way he was holding her—had a look that discouraged empty words. His skin smelt of the sea and the sun.

Judi tried to pull herself together. 'I suppose we managed to get to land. I remember the lifeboat—the panic. Then the calmness of everybody.' She gave what was meant to be a laugh, but it sounded hoarse when it came out, unlike her usual tone. 'It's all mixed up,' she said. 'I don't remember *you*.' Her lips felt numb and she rubbed them with the back of one hand. Then the jostling images began to fall into place.

When the alarms went off she had headed for the companionway with everyone else. There had been some panic, though not a lot at first, though she remembered taking hold of a young girl who had simply frozen to the spot and cajoling her into following the others to the lifeboat stations on one of the upper decks.

Despite the apparent danger, nobody had seemed unduly worried, partly, she suspected, because they didn't really believe anything was seriously wrong. Several people had obviously got straight out of bed and were still wearing their nightclothes and looking round in a bleary fashion. Judi herself, having just finished work and on the point of leaving to go back to her cabin, was still wearing the glittery little scarlet cocktail dress she was so fond of as she'd waited with the others to get into the lifeboat.

None of the passengers on the liner had actually expected to have to go through the whole procedure of abandoning ship. Obviously it was just a drill at a rather inconvenient hour. In fact one man was even threatening to telex a complaint to the chairman of the shipping line first thing in the morning.

Then the ship had suddenly listed. There was a series of explosions, screams, then a deathly hush from everyone as their speculations came to a stop. They had listened as the only sounds to be heard were the grinding of metal and a shuddering roar from deep within the ship. Then the distant shouting of crew members, clear and urgent, had galvanised everyone into action, and after that it was all confusion as people were bundled into the boats in the dark.

It was at this point that the images blurred, and Judi felt another kind of blackness come down as her recollection of what had happened next was obliterated. Now she was somehow here, with this blue-eyed stranger scrutinising her as if not sure whether to believe his eyes or not.

'It's all right,' she gave a croaky laugh. 'I am real.'

'I can see that.' He gave a brief, flashing smile that seemed to send an electric shock right through her body. A small gasp escaped her lips, and his expression changed to one of concern. 'Don't move. Let's make sure you haven't got any broken bones first. There's nothing to move for anyway—we won't be going anywhere for some time.' He gave her a rather baleful glance. 'Can I trust you to stay here for a moment?'

She tried to nod her head, but it hurt too much, and he obviously read the assent in her eyes, for he was suddenly absent and she had to crane painfully round to see where he had gone to.

He was already halfway across the beach that was here only a shelving strip of silver, and she watched him heading towards a ruffle of dark blue-green trees at its summit. When he reached them he disappeared from sight. It made Judi feel very alone. What if he had gone for good? She wanted to get up and run after him, but when she tried to sit up her head began to swim and there was an unbelievable pain in her left leg. Tears suddenly gushed down her cheeks as she registered how helpless she felt. She didn't even know where she was or how she had got here. The beach was totally deserted. Where had everyone else got to? What had happened to the ship? She lifted her glance to the sea, but it was one clear sweep of blue as if coloured in by a single stroke of a painter's brush.

He must have gone to find a road, thought Judi. She began to worry about how she was going to walk. Her leg was throbbing agonisingly and her knee looked twice its usual size. Could a taxi drive down on to the beach to pick her up? Perhaps the man, whoever he was, would call an ambulance? But was she injured enough for that? She probed her left leg, giving an involuntary 'Ouch!' when her fingers touched the tendons. Had she broken something or what? She had no medical knowledge whatsoever. But her rescuer looked practical enough. She remembered his broad, beautiful hands as they moved over her body. There was his firm no-nonsense expression too. She knew he would find someone to look after her.

She patted her hair before sinking back and wondered if it looked as dreadful as it felt. It was like string. Her beautiful sleek bob! Just as soon as she could get to a hairdresser's she would, then everything would be all right. Of course, she wouldn't let just anyone near it, not with a pair of scissors in their hands...

'Come on, wake up! You'll have to walk.'

Hazily Judi opened her eyes. She must have drifted off without realising it. '*Have* to?' She looked up directly into those bright eyes. There was something peremptory about the man that suddenly irritated her. That first glance had disarmed her as she struggled out of oblivion. But she had been looking for reassurance, and he seemed to offer it simply by being there and looking as if he was in charge. But it was only because she had been feeling shaky and confused. Now his manner annoyed her. She wasn't helpless. She wasn't a fool. So who did he think he was? She stayed on the sand and closed her eyes.

'Look, lovely,' came the voice with a note of impatience in it, 'this isn't Tora Tora Beach! Get up. There's some shade further inland.'

She wanted to tell him to go away, but before she could put the words into effect he bent down and gave her a searching glance. 'I know you're feeling fragile, but it's essential to get you into the shade at once. Can you walk?'

'My leg hurts,' she blurted before she could stop herself. There had been a look of real concern in his eyes just then. Sympathy always got through to her when she least expected it. She blinked her eyes a few times to clear the salt water from them. No pity at this stage. She could cope.

'Let's have a look at it,' he said abruptly.

Before she could stop him he bent down and ran both hands expertly over her thighs towards her ankles, and when she flinched and jerked her left leg from beneath his touch as his fingers lightly skimmed it he frowned and took it gently between his palms and studied it. 'Swollen knee—something wrong, obviously. Hope it's not serious.' His expression gave nothing away and he shifted position. Then before she could speak he had hoisted her into his arms and began to carry her up the beach towards the trees.

She was too surprised to speak, and it was a shock when she felt his naked skin, hot and silky and stretched taut over powerful chest muscles, pressing intimately against her own burning flesh. Although he appeared to be quite unaware of what he was doing to her, the sudden physical contact of their near-naked bodies made her tense her muscles in alarm. Her sudden shift of balance made him stumble. 'What's the matter? Am I hurting you?' he growled.

She shook her head, avoiding the eyes which were only inches from her own. There were aquamarine flecks in them, and light blue ones as pale as the sky at dawn, but the light in them was sharp and brilliant, diamantine.

He couldn't have held her more gently as he walked up the beach, but she failed to curb a wriggle, and he said curtly, 'Keep still or I'll drop you.'

'Is that a threat or a promise?' she asked, her throat dry with an unexpected range of emotions dancing through her. He gave her a flashing look from the blue eyes but didn't answer.

She felt herself become boneless, her body responding to him of its own accord, female to male, making her want to cling to him and run her fingers endlessly over the hard, bronzed muscles. I must be in shock, she observed. She didn't usually react like this to complete strangers!

Her head tilted and he observed the slackening of her limbs with a matter-of-fact, 'That's better. When you're tense you become a dead weight.'

Her cheeks burned with the thought that he had guessed what wayward feelings had caused that sudden relaxation, and she tried to keep as still as she could and shut her mind to the fact that he had one arm tight around her waist and the other for support under her bare bottom. Added to that was the fact that it was only the pair of shorts he wore that made him look any different from some glossy magazine centrefold ... She closed her eyes to shut out the sudden image that thundered into her imagination. 'I think if you put me down I can probably walk,' she said stiffly, not looking at him.

'Only a few more metres,' he replied without slackening his grip. He marched on with the same deadpan expression as if it were an everyday occurrence to carry half-naked young women about.

She could see him as a lifeguard in some beach movie without any difficulty.

'Honestly, I think I *can* walk,' she repeated, uncomfortably aware of how she kept slipping and he had to keep on hoisting her up in what seemed like

greater intimacy than ever. She struggled a little,
scared to make matters worse.

'Keep still, will you?' He sounded sick of her
already, and one look at the firm jaw made her
realise how pointless it would be to argue with him.
He was making her feel as helpless as a child. It
was an unusual feeling, for it was usually she who
was in charge.

Fortunately, it was only moments later when he
released her, and though she felt their bodies slide
briefly, burningly, against each other, she managed
to step quickly back out of range. The trouble was,
in her eagerness to get away she forgot her injured
knee, and but for the arm that shot out she would
have fallen. He gripped her hard in an obviously
automatic response, but then he went on holding
her, his eyes, blue as lapis lazuli, fixed expression-
lessly on her upturned face.

'I told you to take it easy,' he said in thickening
tones. 'You're still in shock as well as having a few
physical injuries.' His lips hovered just above her
and she tilted her head, suddenly too weak to do
anything but cling to him. He was strong, something to hold on to. Her fingers trembled as they
moved over the bronze silk of his shoulders. Just
looking into his eyes made her remember the
magical underwater world she had entered when
somebody had taken her out in the glass boat . . . it
was a garden of paradise, with rainbow fish darting
in and out amongst forests of translucent colour—
until that moment when the giant ray had emerged
from the shadows . . . Her eyelashes fluttered and
she came back to the present with a shiver of expectation. He was still holding her. It was as if

neither of them knew what to do next. His face was
very still.

How beautiful he is, she couldn't help regis-
tering. Beautiful but impassive, with a lived-in look,
mature, as if he'd been places. An air of authority
gave depth to his perfect, dark looks. Judi went on
staring helplessly while he held her in his arms.
There were two lines on either side of his mouth—
old laugh lines that sorrow hadn't managed to erase.
Why she thought of sorrow she didn't know, but
she did. She had to fight the impulse to reach up
to them. Other small lines fanned from the outer
corners of his eyes, as if he'd spent a lot of time
staring at the horizon against the sun. And his lips
looked like ones that could touch and be touched—
but in a way that would be forever.

Her own eyes widened, drinking him in, as if
something extraordinary had taken hold of her, but
she couldn't put it into words. Her whole body
seemed to be on fire. Before she could break free
he broke the spell himself. 'Sit here out of the sun,'
he clipped. 'I'm going back to the lifeboat to fetch
some things.' He released her with a gesture that
was impatient to the point of anger.

But at least he helped her hobble the few paces
into the shade of a group of trees. The foliage was
scanty enough, the trunks tall and boughless with
nothing more than a frizz of leaves at their crowns,
but he bent off some low-growing leaves from a
bush for added protection, telling her, 'The sun is
our biggest danger right now. You're already quite
burnt.'

'We'll be all right as soon as we get to a hotel,'
she replied, irritated by the way he had stared so

intently at her and then abruptly pushed her aside as if he had finally decided to give her a negative assessment. Now he was bossing her about. There was a streak of coldness in him, she observed. That type.

She let the leaves drop to the ground, but he picked them up. There was an odd look on his face and she thought he was going to start an argument, but instead he merely said, 'A hotel? Yes, I'm sure you're right. Hang on to that thought.' Then he walked abruptly away towards the water's edge and she lost sight of him as he disappeared round the curve of the beach. There must be a landing-stage further round, she thought, watching for him to reappear. But why then was I lying on the beach when I eventually came round? Who took me there?

She shivered. There were too many unanswered questions now her mind had started to function again. Why, for instance, were they alone together? How had they both got here? Had he deliberately brought her away out of sight of the others? Her palms felt suddenly clammy with the thought that she knew nothing about him. Who was he? He could be any Tom, Dick or Harry. For a moment she had blindly trusted him on the strength of that look of concern when he had inspected her swollen knee. But had he really felt concern? Or was it something else? The memory of how his fingers had skimmed her naked flesh made her shiver again, this time with fear. Her emotions had been instantly hijacked by his sexual charisma. But did danger lie ahead?

It's so lonely here, she observed, looking along the deserted beach again. What if he were some kind of maniac who went in for kidnapping young women to satisfy his own secret purposes?

She forced herself to smile. Even if her legs weren't functioning, her imagination was back in action! Of course he was all right. He was a crewman from the ship, as safe as houses.

Firmly pushing her fantasies aside, she forced herself to her feet and tried an experimental step or two. Wincing with pain, she subsided to the ground. One thing was certain: when he'd said, 'Don't move,' he'd obviously been showing off his sense of humour!

She picked up the banana leaves and stuck them in the sand to form a screen, then settled back in the shade to wait. In hardly any time she saw him trudging back towards her through the blazing sand. There was sweat glistening in the hollows of his chest when he came up and she saw he was lugging a load of things up from the lifeboat. But before he even came to a stop he met a barrage of questions.

'Where are all the others?' she demanded, unable to hold back any longer. 'Are they still near the lifeboat? Why don't they come up here and sit under the shade like me? They're not injured, are they?' Her thoughts flashed to the girl she had tried to help on board the liner and to the people she had been working with, and she wondered if they had all managed to get away in the same boat. 'I can't remember much after climbing down towards the lifeboat,' she added uncertainly. 'What happened? Did I get a crack on the head or something?'

Infuriatingly he took a while to answer. She had to wait until he'd dragged a few more leaves down

and fixed a more substantial sun-screen. When he
sat down beside her she gave him an impatient
glance. 'So how long are we going to sit here? Have
you told somebody I'm going to need help to get
to the road?'

'The road,' he said, and gave her that odd glance
again.

'How far is it? I didn't hear a single car all the
time you were gone.'

'Sound travels, but not that well.'

'How far is it?' she insisted, disturbed now by
his strange manner.

He gave her a crooked grin. 'Coupla thousand
miles, I guess. You thinking of setting out now or
something?'

There was a pause. Judi gazed at him intently,
expecting him to laugh and admit that a car from
one of the hotels was on its way, but he went on
looking at her with his depthless blue eyes as if
trying to plumb her mind. He wanted a reaction,
obviously. Suddenly something snapped. She felt
furious. From feeling weak and helpless when she
looked at him, she swung the other way and her
fists clenched. She gave him one of her coldest
stares.

'Look, I've been damned patient so far, sitting
here half naked under this blazing sun. You've got
me at a disadvantage, with my stupid knee making
it difficult to walk,' her throat constricted, but she
went on, 'I can tell you one thing, Mr Whoever-
the-hell-you-are, I'm not used to being pushed
around. It's hellishly hot here. I'm hungry, tired
and in pain.' She wanted to add, and you've been
too damned familiar, but was afraid of what it

might unleash, so she went on, 'As well as that I'm being bitten to bits by midges and I'm bored to death with all this messing about. I want a nice long shower. And *now*! So stop playing games with me and tell me how long we've got to wait. That's all I'm asking.'

There was a brief pause while he digested all this, then he said, 'I guess you're going to have to learn one thing.'

'What's that?'

His expression didn't alter. 'Patience,' he growled. 'A lot of it.'

'To hell with that,' she retorted. 'I'm not the patient type.'

'Then you'll have to learn,' he replied with brutal finality. He got up. 'I'm going to have a recce further inland.' Without even telling her to stay put as he had done before, he began to stride off.

'Just you come back here!' Judi shouted, and when he kept on walking, she half rose so she was resting on her good knee and using the bole of the tree for support. She screamed after him, '*Come back!* Who the hell do you think you are, ordering me about like this? Don't you *dare* walk off again!' Her voice had risen uncharacteristically and she realised she'd lost control of it. She closed her mouth abruptly, surprised at herself. Was she frightened? There was real fear in her voice. But there was nothing to be frightened of.

At least, that was what she thought until her companion swung round. Then she saw the eyes of ocean-blue ice over and an automatic quiver of apprehension ran through her. She'd gone too far. He was raging. What she had taken for indifference was cold self-control. Inside, beneath that glacial glance, was a tempest of emotion, all of it dangerous, to judge from the way he was regarding her now.

Yet by the time he reached her, it was all iced in again with nothing more dangerous than indifference on his face again. He flicked a glance impersonally over her, then squatted down in front of her, and she watched as, in the manner of someone imparting a lesson to a small child, he told her, 'I wasn't joking about the nearest road. We're not in a joking situation.' He scrutinised her face for a sign of reaction, then, apparently reassured, went on. 'You've got to know the truth. You may as well have it now. But I warn you, I'm not good with hysterical women.'

'I'm not the hysterical type,' she clipped through suddenly stiff lips. What was he trying to tell her? Why that guarded look on his face as if he didn't want to admit to something? 'Tell me,' she persisted.

He paused. 'Well, lovely,' his voice dropped an interval, 'I think you'd better tell me your name first.'

'Why?' she managed to stutter.

'Because we're going to have to spend some time together.'

'Are we?' she managed to whisper. Unconsciously she wrapped her arms more tightly around her naked breasts. She had almost forgotten about her lack of clothes, but now all her earlier fantasies reared up, as lurid as ever. Was she his prisoner after all? But she would escape, and he'd better believe it. She gave him a skidding glance from beneath her lashes.

'Well?' he prompted when she didn't supply an answer immediately.

'I'm called Judi,' she said as curtly as she could.

'You weren't a passenger, were you?'

She shook her head. 'What the hell's it got to do with you? What's your name, anyway?'

He gave her a smile that was a mere tightening of his jaw. There was a slight hesitation before he said, 'Call me Dan.'

'Well, Dan,' she said, regaining some of her composure with an effort. 'That's the social side of things sorted out.'

'Now for the reality,' he cut in harshly. 'When the ship blew up last night we were the lucky ones. We were the ones who got away. Let's hope we weren't the only ones.' He paused, and Judi realised now that his face was sombre with signs of an immense strain. That fact, even more than his words, made her flesh begin to creep. It prepared her in some way for what he told her next.

'When I fished you out of the water,' he went on, 'you were tangled up among some wreckage, otherwise you'd have drowned, because, as you've guessed, you were knocked unconscious. We were swept away from the ship. It was too black to see anything. I managed to locate the flares, but they didn't help.' He seemed to consider his words for a moment, then he said, 'We beached here through sheer good luck. Or did we?' He examined her expression. 'How much can you take?'

'How—what do you mean?' she asked, cold fear stilling her thoughts.

'We're alone, on a rock atoll. We don't know whether there's fresh water or not. Or where we are, whether on the main shipping routes or somewhere...' he smiled wryly '...less frequented.'

Judi opened her lips, then closed them again.

'OK, that's enough,' he said abruptly. 'I'm going to have a look round.' He rose to his full height, the simple movement showing how commanding he was, and she was even more aware of it now he was her only hope of survival.

Shudders of fright swept up and down her, but she managed to give him a smile. 'I'll wait right here,' she tried to joke, indicating her swollen knee. She held her breath until he was out of sight among the trees. He hadn't looked back. He hadn't smiled. He hadn't said anything to reassure her.

As soon as she was alone she began to gasp, tearless with fear, scarcely able to get her breath, fingers clawing at the sand on either side of her, her heels digging into the ground as if she could burrow her way to safety that way. As soon as the first spasm had passed she forced her mind into gear.

She mustn't give way—that was the first thing. It would turn out all right. There would be search parties. A cruise liner as big as theirs couldn't go down without a full-scale search being mounted. Soon there would be helicopters overhead. Before that they would probably find a road on the other side of the island—a hotel, even. No island was completed deserted these days, not even in the Pacific. The world was one big tourist resort. People were always complaining that it was impossible to find anywhere unspoilt nowadays. The more she thought about it the more she convinced herself it was true.

He, Dan, was simply trying to scare her.

Some men were like that. It made them feel macho if they could appear cool in a crisis. He was the type that would revel in taking control when everything seemed to be falling apart.

She would show him she wasn't impressed by games like that. When he came back she would be totally in control, just like him. She would be a block of ice.

CHAPTER TWO

THE shadow cast by Dan's sun-screen was almost non-existent, and Judi had to drag herself deeper into the band of trees above the beach in an effort to find some protection from the overhead sun. The blue-green foliage, so enticing from the shore, was too sparse close up to be much protection. As far as she could see there was nothing beyond the trees except scrub and short, stubby, prickly-looking plants whose names she didn't know.

She felt close to despair. It had been over an hour since Dan had left and her imagination was working overtime with what might have happened to him. She pictured treacherous ravines, Dan falling over and over to the rocks below. She saw savage animals of some kind, fangs bared to tear him limb from limb, or hostile settlers, stalking him with loaded guns until they'd cornered him in some blind valley, for something must have happened to keep him away so long... She trailed sand through her fingers and forced herself to keep calm and think of ice blocks. Propping her injured leg up, she forced her imagination into some kind of order, methodically going through the more likely reasons for his delay.

Perhaps he's got lost, she thought. Maybe the island is bigger than we think. He's organising help. That takes time. Everything's all right. It's simply taking time to get things done.

Then she dozed a little and the dreams started, this time mixed up with the nightmare of the sinking ship, and she relived the moment until everything blanked out, but this time it went on, and there were ravening animals closing in on them, rising up out of the raging seas, and then a ravine, unaccountably dry, into which she and Dan were falling, turning over and over as they plummeted to earth...

Her eyes snapped open. He was back. She saw him reaching down for her, saw his strong arms on either side of her shoulders. '*Oh, God!* Thank heavens you're here!' Tears gushed independently from her eyes before she could stop them, then before she knew what she was doing she was reaching up to him, clutching him round the neck, pulling him into her arms in a fever of need. It was only when her lips touched the side of his mouth that she knew she had gone too far. The contact brought her abruptly to her senses. He had already drawn back.

'I'm sorry, I didn't mean that...' Her hands fell away. 'I don't know why I did that,' she muttered, cold with embarrassment. 'I was asleep and——' She remembered what he'd said about hysterical women and closed her mouth.

He ignored the whole incident, saying briskly, 'How's the knee? Can you walk yet? There's shelter over the other side among the rocks. I think I can even rig up a kind of den for the night.'

Judi gave him a darting glance. 'No road or houses...?'

He shrugged. 'Why should there be? This is just a stump of rock.'

The full horror of their situation descended again, and she felt numbed by the thought that they were trapped, but Dan was impatient to get moving. 'Come on, let's go. We have a lot to organise by nightfall.'

He helped her to her feet and she tried a step or two, but, even though she vowed she could walk if she took it slowly, he insisted on carrying her again. This time she managed to control her desire to press her lips to his, knowing how unwelcome such forwardness would be, and with frequent stops over the rough ground they managed to get to the other side of the island.

'It really is just a rock,' she observed when they came to a halt on an outcrop on the windward side. She moved away from Dan so that she wasn't clinging to his arm as she felt urged to. With a sensible distance between them both she said, 'We could have drifted in the boat for days without finding this place. Lucky we got here.' She tried to give a smile to show she was in control—fortunately he seemed to have forgotten the earlier episode—but, instead of agreeing with her, he merely looked thoughtful and scratched the side of his chin. Then he gave a short laugh as if she had said something funny and turned away.

'What is it…?' She paused. 'Dan…?' she added, feeling that by using his name she was crossing some Rubicon. Despite the physical intimacy of being carried they were as distanced from each other as two strangers at a cocktail party. But he didn't seem to notice, and when he turned towards her she felt he was thinking of something entirely different. She watched his expression as he seemed to weigh something in his mind. Then he said,

'Luck, you said? You call it luck, lady?' He gave a shrug of impatience and turned and began to head for the rocks further down.

Judi felt so thoroughly annoyed by his manner that it almost swamped her fears and discomforts. Was it that patronising 'lady' that did it? His whole attitude to her was disparaging. As if he just didn't want to be bothered with her. Just who did he think he was? It wasn't her fault she was injured and couldn't do anything useful. Now he was playing about among the rocks, totally oblivious to her, simply messing about like a small boy. She supposed she was expected to go down and ask him what he was doing. Well, she was damned if she was going to.

She found a shaded place and tried to make herself comfortable, but the rocks weren't designed for sitting on. They were covered with small, sharp encrustations, and she shifted from place to place, her knee throbbing like mad, her temper rising, and still Dan didn't come back and explain what he was doing. All she could see was his dismissive, naked back, turned against her.

She watched him. He was heaving stones about, piling them up at the bottom of the slope. There was no sense in it. If he was building some sort of cairn he was mad. They should be on the other side of the island watching for passing ships, not fooling about amongst a heap of stones where nobody could see them.

*   *   *

'Is it at all possible you could make yourself useful?' cut in a voice, scattering her thoughts and bringing her bolt upright where she sat.

'I beg your pardon?' Judi rubbed the back of a grubby hand over her eyes.

Dan towered over her, his face streaked with sweat, the muscles of his back glistening as he turned in the sun. Even like this he was beautiful and must know it. She averted her glance.

He said, 'You could brew up a mug of tea, perhaps? Injuries permitting?'

He seemed about to stamp off up the slope again—the top of it now crowned by the pile of stones, she noticed, like a funnel—when she bit out, 'I'd love nothing more. But how I'm supposed to provide tea I don't know. Wave a wand, perhaps?'

He gave her a lop-sided grin. 'Didn't you see me bring the stuff from the boat up here? You must have been dozing again.' His glance went beyond her and when she turned she bit her lip, for he was right, she really must have been asleep, for he had brought up some of the equipment from the lifeboat.

'I didn't see it,' she said stiffly. 'I can't understand why I'm sleeping such a lot.'

'Sort it out, will you?' He nodded briefly, and once again she had to watch him stalk off with that arrogant pelvic swagger as if he owned the place...

Fuming, she hobbled over to the gear from the boat and rummaged amongst it. There was a sort of temporary survival kit—a small Primus stove, a drypack of matches, basic medical supplies, a water container, vitamin pills, some packets of dried food, sachets of tea and coffee and dried milk. Kneeling precariously on her good leg, Judi set the Primus on a flattish stone and crouched over it, cupping one of the matches as she struck it against the rock. But when she turned the knob on the Primus nothing happened.

At that moment Dan came up, saw what she was doing and gave a muffled curse. 'Try filling it with fuel.' She glanced over her shoulder to see him turning away again. Feeling like a fool, she searched among the rest of the stuff, located what she should have noticed to begin with, and set the stove up properly. This time when he came back she had the small tin kettle singing merrily.

She handed him a beaker of tea. 'I assume you wanted tea and not coffee,' she said.

He took it with a nod of thanks. 'Last of the luxuries. We'll have to deal with the water problem next.'

'How do you mean?' She stifled her hurt at the way he had taken the tea from her with scarcely a glance.

'There ain't none,' he said humorously. 'Know how long we can live without water?'

'About . . .' she searched her mind for an almost forgotten scrap of information '. . . five days?'

He nodded. 'Something like that. But don't worry, you're with me.'

She let out a squeak of laughter. 'I find that most reassuring.'

He sat down beside her. 'Tell me about yourself,' he invited. The blue eyes skidded over her tanned face, but, before she could recover from the brief feeling that at last he was giving her the attention she deserved, he went on, 'I mean in respect of any useful skills you might happen to have.'

'Skills?' Judi raised her eyebrows. She thought of a failed typing course, the cordon bleu cookery lessons her mother had insisted on, riding, skiing... 'What sort of skills?'

'Practical survival skills.' Dan looked at her in a cold, objective way that made her feel thoroughly assessed—and dismissed. Useless. He thought she was useless, she could tell.

'Is it because I'm female you look at me as if I'm no good for anything?' she demanded in a tight voice.

'Some women are eminently useful,' he came back. 'Unfortunately I don't think you're one of them.'

'Why should I be? I didn't get us into this mess.' She turned away to avoid his glance. That wasn't what she had meant to say. It made her sound querulous, like a spoilt child. But Dan seemed to bring out the negative in her. 'Why did you laugh when I said it was lucky we'd beached here?' she asked.

'Because if we'd been able to drift with the current we might have fetched up in the shipping lanes again, with more chance of help.'

'Why don't we just get back into the boat and drift, then?' she asked cuttingly. He seemed to delight in making things more difficult than they were.

'Because, my dear girl,' he said in his most patronising tone, 'the boat's a write-off. We hit a coral reef and were damn lucky to get ashore at all.' He paused. 'I hoped we might be able to fix it to get us to sea again, but there are problems with that idea.'

'Then solve them!' she retorted. 'You seem to have appointed yourself commander-in-chief.'

'I'll assume it's fear that makes you talk like that, not sheer pigheaded arrogance.'

'What?' Nobody had ever spoken to her like this before. She wanted to draw herself up and tell him who she was, but for a moment anger made her speechless. He was just some conceited crewman from the liner, and because he thought he knew all about survival he thought he had the right to treat her with contempt.

She said, 'If you think you're so clever, I suggest you get us off this God-forsaken place as soon as possible. I don't think I'm going to be able to take much more of you. We're total opposites.'

His lips tightened contemptuously. 'You're not on board now with a stream of flunkeys dancing attendance, lovey.'

She gave him a thin smile. 'I've already told you, I wasn't a passenger. I was working on board that ship.'

'As?'

Judi turned away.

'Pity you weren't on the nursing staff. Now that would have been useful. Or catering, even.' Dan cocked an eyebrow, forcing her to mumble an answer.

When he heard what she said his reaction was exactly what she expected. His laugh couldn't have been more scathing. 'The resident DJ? *Great!* My luck really is in! At least you could fix the elec-

trics—if there were any. Or did you always leave
that sort of thing to some besotted follower or two?'

'You don't have to be so bloody rotten to me!'
she burst out. 'How many other normal people
would know what to do in a situation like this?
Nobody expects a cruise liner to blow up in mid-
ocean! How could you expect me to be prepared
for a thing like that? And anyway, you were in the
boat as well as me, and at least you weren't unconscious. You should have made sure we stayed
near the ship and not been swept away out of sight
of it. At least then we'd have had a chance of being
picked up! It's all your fault! And you're just trying
to make me feel bad because you know you're to
blame!'

Dan didn't bother to reply. Instead he simply got
to his feet and walked off out of earshot. If she
could have got up too she would have. She would
have run after him and made him turn to face her,
forced a response out of him, for anything, even
open antagonism, was better than this blank indifference to her. Then when she'd done that, she'd
have gone to the opposite side of the island, made
a signal fire, and got herself rescued and to hell
with him!

As it was, she was stuck. She began to shiver
despite the sun beating down, heating the rocks on
which she sat. She knew it was fear, not cold, for
what if they were never spotted? For all their
wrangling the stark truth was constantly there beneath the surface. How easy would it be for a plane
to spot them? They ought to do something that
would make them visible from the air instead of
sitting here arguing. She drew up her legs and

rocked from side to side. Her limbs would not stop trembling.

Dan had come back and now he reached across and looped one arm round her shoulders. 'It's going to be all right,' he said briskly. 'You're still in shock. Drink up your tea. Is there plenty of sugar in it?'

'I don't take sugar,' she informed him, trying to draw away from the enveloping arm.

'Then this time you must.'

'I don't like it.'

'Forget your figure. You may have a chance to lose more weight than you bargained for—if that's what's bothering you.' He moved away and found the packs of dried goods, poured two sachets of sugar into her mug and topped it up again. 'Drink it.'

For a moment Judi mistook his action for kindness, but he soon disillusioned her. 'You're more use fit and well than cracking up on me. I'm going to need your help later on. We're going to have to work as a team to survive this place. Understand? That means pulling together.' His blue eyes lazed over her face. 'Forget personal animosities; they're a luxury we can't afford. One of us sick will bring the other down with them. Now I'm going to tell you what to do.'

Here we go again, she thought rebelliously, but what he had said made sense. Sipping the tea, she felt her nerves calm a little, and as he outlined his plans she realised she was lucky to have fetched up with a man who seemed to know what he was talking about. Lucky he was one of the crew and not a passenger—she doubted whether any of the overweight, rich old men or their over-painted wives

who comprised most of the passenger-list would
have even got them this far. Grudgingly, she put
herself into servant mode and for the next few hours
was at his beck and call.

Night dropped over them as suddenly as a black
lid. Then the tropical sky was awash with stars.
Working hard for the rest of the day, Dan had
hauled wood up to the chimney he had built and
as soon as it was dark had set it alight. As a beacon
it was a great success. 'All it needs,' he told Judi
with a wry smile, 'is someone to see it.'

While he had been doing that he set her to
trimming branches to make a shelter to protect them
from both wind and sun. Then she'd had to use his
knife—why had he been carrying a knife?—to trim
more branches to lie on that night. 'We could sleep
on the beach,' he told her, 'but I'd rather stay near
the beacon to make sure it doesn't go out. You can
sleep down there if you like, it'll be more
comfortable.'

The thought of lying alone on some deserted
beach filled her with all kinds of fears and she
quickly shook her head. 'It's all right. I'll take turns
at stoking the beacon.'

He looked surprised. 'Maybe I'll let you do that
once you can walk around properly,' he agreed. The
dismissive nod he gave made her feel useless again.
She surveyed her broken nails and the weals on the
palms of her hands where she had had to tug at the
thick branches and thought how unfair he was to
her. She was doing her best. He had treated her like
a slave all day and she had gone along with it as
meekly as could be. But it still didn't please him.

He had it fixed in his head that she was nothing but a liability.

Let him think what he likes, she grumbled to herself as she tumbled into a tired heap on the bed of brackeny stuff they had heaped up for the night. Soon they would be freed from their island prison and, not soon enough, from each other. She shivered and tried to pull some of the leaves over her, but they didn't act as insulation as she'd hoped. The temperature seemed to have dropped dramatically.

'Dan,' she said after about an hour of tossing and turning, 'can't we use that piece of polythene from the boat to lie under? It would be like being in a tent.'

She had seen him carrying it back towards the beach before turning in for the night. He grunted some non-committal reply and she reached over and shook him by the shoulder. *'Dan?'* she insisted. In the darkness she saw him lift his head. His hair seemed to reflect the light from somewhere, star-shine perhaps, for there was no moon. An irrational impulse to run her fingers through it made her roll away so she didn't have to look. He was horrible, the worst sort of man. And because he was the only one around she had to start fancying him! What a joke! When she got back to civilisation she would tell Tia and Jane and they would have a good laugh about the unpredictability of the sexual urge.

'The most *boorish* man you can imagine!' she would say. 'God help me, I didn't know which was worst, the prospect of drowning at sea or being trapped on an island with *him*!' She could imagine their comments. 'And then,' she would say with a dismissive laugh, 'I actually started to feel a little bit randy! I suppose it was the stress. Desert islands sound romantic, and you know what my imagination is like!'

They would all have a good giggle and she would add, 'Thank heavens I'm not the type to lose my self-control!' The girls would put him in perspective, reduce him to the insignificant mortal he really was.

Now she knew he was awake because she could feel him looking at her, but he hadn't even bothered to reply. Right, she thought, she would *make* him reply.

Jerking upright, she said loudly, 'Look, tell me where the damned polythene is and I'll fetch it myself. I can't lie here like this all night. I'm bloody cold. I want to get some sleep.'

She heard him shift and imagined she could see two pin-bright eyes boring into her. Then out of the darkness came his bleared voice. 'I would have thought you'd had enough sleep today—you haven't done much else. Now do you mind if I get some?'

His words cut her to the quick. She could still feel the lacerations of those wretched palm fronds or whatever they were that had had to be cut to make their so-called bed. 'I've done my share!' she exploded. 'Is it my fault I can't run around like a lunatic?'

'If that's what you intend to do when your knee's better maybe I'd better see to the other one for you.'

'God, you're *heartless*!' she spat. 'I'm not wasting time in this!' She scrambled on to one knee and was about to stand up when she felt two hands like iron clamps round her naked waist.

'Where the hell are you going?' came the bleary voice again. 'Keep still and go to sleep.'

'I've told you, I'm getting the polythene to sleep under. You seem to forget I've only got this skimpy bit of material round me.' It had dawned on her that she was wearing what remained of her favourite disco dress, and the lord alone knew what had happened to the rest of it. A few sequins still clung to the filmy material. It was hardly adequate protection against the night.

'Listen, sugar,' Dan's tone had sharpened and she had obviously roused him from his slumbers, 'you're not going anywhere, least of all to touch that polythene. You want water, don't you? Where do you think we're going to get it?'

'There's some in the container,' she replied.

'And how long is that likely to last?' he persisted, eyeing her closely.

She tried to prise his hands from around her waist, but he seemed equally determined to hold on.

'I'll tell you how long it'll last,' he said into the silence. 'Two days at most.'

Remembering what had been said earlier, Judi could think of no immediate reply, but when he didn't say anything else she asked, trying at the same time to disguise the dread in her voice, 'So we have to get water somehow?' He must have rigged up some sort of contraption with the polythene. She didn't understand how, but she couldn't let him know that. In a small voice she asked, 'How long do you think we might be stranded here?'

She felt his grip tighten for a moment, but his voice was casual when he said, 'Who knows? Maybe only a few days. Don't worry too much about that. Just learn to think ahead.'

'You mean prepare for a long stay?'

Was that what he had been doing all day? Planning ahead? Thinking in terms of the worst scenario—and not even panicking?

'I hadn't thought of it like that,' she told him, unable to avoid a grudging tone. He wrong-footed her all the time, whatever she did or said.

'Now you can.' He released her and she sank miserably back amongst the prickly leaves.

'Come here,' he murmured. 'We have the best insulating materials in the world. Let's be sensible and make use of them.'

'What's that?' she asked, not moving, though he seemed to be trying to drag her towards him.

'Each other,' he said succinctly.

'Don't you *dare*——!' she protested as his grip tightened round her.

'It's all right, I'm too exhausted for any hanky-panky. Besides,' he added, laughing softly, 'you're not my type.'

'Nor you mine,' Judi retorted, but when he simply increased the pressure she found herself being drawn irresistibly into his embrace, and the way her body responded was proof of the lie. Trying not to let him know how wild were the desires he aroused, she allowed him to take her in his arms, and they clung together, their bodies fitting naturally, mutual body warmth gradually easing them both into sleep.

'Like babes in the wood,' she heard him murmur in a sleep-hazed voice as he drifted off.

Some babe! she thought. Halfway to heaven, she at last allowed her fingers to lose themselves in the thicket of blue-black hair.

CHAPTER THREE

THEY had been working together throughout the morning, clearing the ground of scrub in the middle of the island to reveal the greyish rock beneath. Dan had measured it out, first pacing a rough shape as close to the size of a football pitch as he could and placing marker stones at each corner, then instructing Judi to start scraping the rock clear in a wide swathe between the markers.

At first she tried using her bare hands, pulling at the scrub and trying to yank it out by the roots, but, when this proved ineffective, she found a sharp stone and hacked away until she found the knack of cutting at the roots, rolling it back like turf, then scraping with the edge of the stone until it was clear.

It was time-consuming and in the heat of the day a painful and unpleasant task, but it had to be done. It didn't need Dan to explain why, for as she had already figured it herself, if they could make a sign visible to any passing spotter plane they would stand more chance of being rescued.

It took most of the day working down one line, then another and another, until finally they met somewhere in the middle. Dan, busy elsewhere for part of the day, had started later than Judi had, but soon cleared the far end and completed one of the diagonals, and now they surveyed their accomplishments with tired satisfaction.

'How's the knee?' he demanded without looking up when he got within speaking range.

'The swelling seems to have gone down. I don't think anything was broken. It must have been only a strain after all.' She had found witch-hazel in the medical kit, and the application of a cotton-wool compress seemed to have done the trick. It was what the housekeeper had done when she had wrenched an ankle in a fall from her pony as a child. She didn't tell Dan this because she knew he wouldn't care a damn. All he wanted to know was whether she was fit enough to carry out the next task he had lined up for her. Because for sure there would be one.

She frowned down at her hands for a moment. Her nails were broken right off now and looked dreadful. If she ever got back to civilisation she would have to go to nail school. Tia would fly to New York with her—no more ships for her—and they would have a shopping spree, really binge themselves. Yes, if ever she climbed back out of this terrible nightmare, that was what she would do.

'OK?' Dan had drawn level, working at twice her speed, of course. But then he didn't have to put most of his weight on only one leg. He dropped his stone digger and for a moment she thought he was going to say something encouraging, but all he said was, 'Think you can finish off by yourself?'

She nodded miserably.

When she next looked up she was alone again. Perhaps if it had been anyone else she might have suspected him of sloping off for a rest—the pace he was setting was inhuman—but she knew he

wouldn't do a thing like that. He was the most en-
ergetic man she had ever met, including her own
father. Ferociously single-minded, he hadn't
stopped from opening his eyes in the morning to
closing them at night. He was a one-man power-
house, making no allowances for her, and, she had
to admit it, none for himself either.

Grudgingly she acknowledged that a little bit of
his arrogance was justified. Things had got done.
There was a purpose now. The hopelessness she had
felt to begin with, when she had slowly understood
the situation they were in, had been transformed
into a single, positive determination to be rescued.
Dan's own sheer will-power had been the driving
force. But he would be hell to live with in real life,
she surmised, and she had begun to wonder about
that. How could such a man be happy as a mere
crewman on a liner? What sort of scope was there
in a job like that for the initiative and drive he
seemed to possess in such abundance?

Everything about him was still a mystery. His
manner didn't encourage small talk. They had
scarcely spoken about anything other than practical problems in the three days that had elapsed
since first being stranded. At first Judi had felt it
was because there simply hadn't been time. Now
she wondered if it was because he couldn't be
bothered to talk to her about anything that wasn't
going to get them back to safety. He had said she
wasn't his type. That included time-wasting conversation with her too, it seemed.

With a heart like lead she completed the aerial
sign, surveying the large white cross their efforts
had effected with a sort of fatalistic smile as she

turned away. Now it was all in the hands of whoever watched over castaways to send a rescue plane for them.

She limped back towards base camp, which was what they had got into the habit of calling the heap of palm leaves, now much crushed by three restless nights, and the cooking fire round which most of the time not working was spent. They never lit the fire until nightfall, the days were too hot, and then it was done merely to conserve the fuel in the Primus and to ensure they had some means of keeping the beacon alight should it go out. There was only a finite number of matches in the now much-depleted survival kit, Dan had pointed out.

'You're looking glum,' he said when she came up. The kettle was on and he was mixing something odd-looking in a bowl.

'No, I'm pleased,' she said, flopping down on the palm-leaf bed. 'Delighted and deranged by pleasure!' It was true. She felt light-headed every time she looked at his handsome face, for despite what she thought about him he still did strange things to her emotions. But she was hardly going to tell him that.

He gave her a glance and she emitted a short laugh. 'It's all right, I'm not cracking up. It's just that that was a hell of a job and I'm glad it's over.'

'You've done well,' he replied, peering into the bowl and therefore failing to notice her start of surprise.

Praise from the commander, she thought, then bit the words back. He would probably turn it around so that it wasn't after all the compliment it sounded. Obviously he was being ironic. Or doing the right thing in his role of chief and trying to keep up the morale of the troops.

Judi gazed bitterly out to sea. There was no reason for his coldness. She'd done nothing to provoke it, but by now it was obvious that he was only ever going to treat her impersonally. From where she was sitting the sea looked limitless, and whichever way she turned she could see only the circular rim of an empty world with them as its centre. Above their heads the blue of a heaven quite indifferent to their fate shut them in. Her spirits were like lead. No one would ever find them, and the man she was trapped with didn't care a damn for her.

She felt as if there was nothing left to live for. No one knew where they were. By now they must have been written off with the missing from the liner. That was all there was to be said. Thoughts of her mother and how she would take the news brought tears to her eyes. How would her father and her sister Sarah react? It was bad that she'd left them like that—not the way she wanted them to remember her at all. She wondered if they would remember her kindly now she was as good as dead.

'Come on, cheer up!' Dan broke into her self-recriminations. 'I've made us something special for supper.'

She tried to raise some interest. 'What is it?'

'That's the one thing you mustn't ask.' His blue eyes crinkled teasingly, but when she instantly returned his smile he switched off again.

'I suppose my next task is to be food-taster-in-chief?' she said abruptly, pretending not to be hurt by his lack of friendliness. 'If I turn green at the gills you'll know it's poison.' She felt so depressed that she almost hoped it was.

'Would I do a thing like that to you?' he asked. But before she could take it as a tiny sign of warmth he added, 'You're fifty per cent of the work-force—worth your weight. Come on, try it. I can guarantee it's first-class protein. Just what we need to perk us up.' He held a mug out to her at arm's length.

She took it and inspected it with a look of exaggerated misgivings. 'I don't want to feel perked up. I simply want to slide into oblivion,' she said as she took an exploratory mouthful. She handed it back with a grimace. 'It seems to lack that certain something,' she observed. Dan came to sit beside her, unexpectedly putting an arm around her shoulders. Concealing her surprise, she tried not to show how his body against her own summoned an immediate and soul-searing reaction. Instead she fixed her eyes on the way the fingers of his right hand grazed her bare forearm, measuring the contrast in their skin tones as a way of keeping her mind off more lascivious thoughts.

Already they were both a deep honey-hazel shade. Judi was pleased she wasn't the fair-skinned type. His tan was a fraction deeper than her own, and together their skin looked good. She was still unused to the fact that she was having to wander around practically stark naked. What had happened to her panties when Dan rescued her? She had formed the picture of him pulling her naked body from the waves, having cut her free from the entangling wreckage as he had described. It was a voluptuous image, and what must he have felt as he dragged her practically nude body into the lifeboat? She couldn't imagine. Nothing, it seemed. He was made of stone. All she wanted was a show of affection, to be held a little in his arms. He was a machine, oblivious and uncaring that she was frightened half out of her life most of the time. She adjusted the slip of scarlet, sequin-scattered voile and tried to tell herself that with a tan she was almost respectably dressed.

Dan added a few more touches to the gunge he expected her to eat, then sat down beside her again. 'Listen, lovely,' he squeezed her shoulders, breaking into her ruminations, 'you're not sliding into oblivion just yet, so don't even think it.'

She moved out of the crook of his arm as if shifting more comfortably, but it was really to get away from him. She knew she was falling deeper under his spell with every day that passed, and it wasn't oblivion she was sliding into, it was hell . . . because he just didn't feel the same way. What was worse was that on the odd occasions when he did show some interest it made it even more difficult to want to keep him at a safe distance. Not that she had a real choice. He just didn't want to get close. His mind was on survival and nothing else.

He handed the result of his culinary experiment to her on one of the edible leaves of wild lettuce they had discovered, and she put some in her mouth and chewed. His eyes were piercing bright, waiting for her verdict with keen interest. 'Not bad,' she announced with a guarded smile. 'It tastes sort of fishy. Actually . . .' she chewed again, ' . . . quite nice.' To be honest, she was ravenous, and anything that

wasn't dry tack from the survival rations was like
manna from heaven.

'I managed to catch some fish this morning while
you were busy scraping on the hill,' Dan told her.
'We won't starve after all.' His eyes roamed her
face for signs of alarm.

'I hadn't thought we'd starve,' she blurted,
feeling the fear return.

'That's because you hadn't thought,' he came
back in his usual cold voice. 'Luckily there's an
abundance of good fish around these waters. The
only problem is how to catch the devils.'

'How do you know they're edible?' she asked,
stifling the hurt she felt when he dismissed her as
empty-headed as usual. 'Well,' she answered her
own question, 'I suppose you *would* know that sort
of thing, being a seaman. Aren't I in luck?' she
added bitterly. 'I don't know one fish from another
unless it's salmon, oysters or caviare.' Might as well
play up to the image he has of me, she thought;
why not? Whatever she did or said he would never
think any better of her.

But he was laughing. It was the most relaxed
she'd seen him, and she wished it were because of
something right she'd done or said, but it wasn't.
It was a smile at her expense again. 'You've no idea
how my heart dropped,' he said, 'when you told
me who you were. I suppose I should have known
you were one of the DJs, but I never got around
to going to the disco.'

'I didn't know crew were allowed to mix with the
passengers anyway. We certainly weren't——'

'You must have been disappointed when you discovered that.' He was tucking into the fishy con-

coction himself now, but the way he had changed
the thrust of their idle remarks aroused her interest.

'You weren't an officer, by any chance, were
you?' She frowned. It would be like him to hold
out on her out of sheer cussedness. 'I sort of assumed you were a crewman because of your——'
She broke off. Because of your fantastic physique,
she had been going to say, but that was the last
thing she wanted him to hear.

'Because why?' He peered at her, his face tough
and intelligent, black brows straight as a die, eyes
blue as heaven.

'Because you seem so practical,' she explained
weakly.

He grinned, not quite meeting her glance. 'Can't
officers be practical too?'

'I thought they were all public-school men or
something, leaving the practical stuff to others and
merely learning how to issue orders. Somewhat like
you in that respect, of course.' Judi managed a smile
to take the sting out of her words. 'I don't know
much about that sort of thing anyway.'

He didn't tell her whether her guess was correct
or not, but reverted to his former question. 'What
made you take a job in a ship's disco? Surely it
would have been more comfortable ashore? Or did
you hope to pick up some rich husband en route?'

'Is that what you think of me?' You needn't
answer that, she thought miserably. She knew what
he thought already. 'It's a neat scheme, you have
to admit. And why not? There were some very rich
men on board.'

'Mostly with their lady wives,' he added drily,
watching her, apparently at ease, but his eyes, soul-

lessly blue, like shutters over his real feelings. 'Or maybe that didn't bother you?' he went on, still watching her. 'Maybe you planned to entice one of them into your own life?'

Judi was struck dumb for a moment by this sudden revelation of what he secretly thought of her. It explained why he was so distant towards her. But it was unjust. It was horrible. She felt tears of anger and something else sting behind her eyes, but she gave a nonchalant shrug. 'Sure,' she agreed. 'Why not? Everybody does it. It's an age-old method of securing a rich and happy future.' She added flippantly, 'First find the man—it doesn't matter whose.' She inspected her nails. 'Why shouldn't I like nice things? I like luxury, and life on board was nice, lots of flunkeys, as you call them. I like being waited on. Nothing to do all day except sunbathe, socialise, and, in the evenings, play a few of my favourite sounds while being paid. To top it off with a nice rich husband seems like a recipe for heaven to me. And you ask why I chose to work on board ship rather than ashore? What a question! You've said it all.' She was trembling with fury inside, but Dan would be the last person to discover that. She flicked back a lock of hair and gave him a smooth smile.

He sat back. There was a new expression on his face, as if something unexpected had come into his mind. 'I knew I'd seen you before,' he said at last. He leaned forward. 'It's just dawned on me who you are. It was when you smiled at me just now in that coquettish sort of way...' He paused. 'Hard-boiled as old boots.' He gave that cold smile again. 'You can look quite vulnerable without make-up,

but in full war-paint you're a different prop-
osition.' He gave her a knowing glance. 'You used
the name Kiss Doran ... And I caught sight of you
one evening, but you looked so different from the
way you do now I didn't recognise you.'

'What do you mean?' Judi was puzzled.
Whatever realisation had struck Dan obviously
boded no good for her. She hated the all-knowing
way he was looking at her; it was worse than his
disparaging remarks just now. Did it mean he was
going to become even more unfriendly—if that were
possible? She was cringing too as she remembered
the name Kiss Doran! It had seemed a good idea
to jazz up her image like that—plain Judi de Burgh
didn't sound like a DJ exactly. But really—Kiss
Doran! Whatever had she been thinking of? She
looked at him. 'Well, go on,' she challenged.

'You were in the dining-room,' he said, eyes half
closed as if summoning up the image, 'and wearing
some crazy little glittery outfit with spiky high-
heeled sandals. You were showing off a pair of quite
noticeable legs, you hair an immaculate black bob,
red talons, blood-red lips—hard, glossy, so very
chic ... And one of our more elderly male passengers was popping a strawberry into your open
mouth while his wife looked on.'

His eyes glittered over her face with accusation,
as if she'd been committing some kind of crime instead of being merely flirtatious! What a strait-laced
type he was turning out to be!

But he was going on. 'Your make-up at that point
was faultless and had obviously been applied not
five minutes before in one of our beauty
salons——' He suddenly broke off, but the in-

sulting way he had just described her didn't allow her to wonder why.

She lifted cold eyes to his, tears of hurt anger pressed back into the deepest well of emotion, and said, 'I'm really not your type at all, am I? I guess you'd prefer to see a woman in raggy jeans and a grubby T-shirt, with dirt under her fingernails and untrimmed hair, and of course not a sinful scrap of make-up on her well-scrubbed face!'

Her lips tightened and she felt acutely conscious that she was sitting in front of him with little else but a scrap of voile concealing her body from his accusing gaze, but she fought off the beginnings of a blush and went on, 'That's your type, isn't it, Dan? Plain and down-to-earth, with a mind to match. Eminently useful, as you'd put it. Well, I'd say *boring*. A woman who can drudge for you all day without a murmur of complaint.'

Which is exactly what *I've* been doing for the last three days, she told herself in silent outrage.

'*Your* type,' she went on scathingly, 'are the so-called salt of the earth—at least that's what men like you call them. Because they're self-effacing slaves, and that's all you want. A woman without a mind of her own. With no pride, beauty or wit.' Her voice choked suddenly and she coughed to clear it. It was the worst torment of all to know there was nowhere to run to, to get away from him, to escape this relentless and horribly unfair judgement.

He was silent for a moment and reached forward to drop a stick on the fire. When he looked at her he sounded quite amused. 'Of all the two people on board we must be the most ill-matched pair of the lot. Still, you mustn't let it get to you. I'll have

us rescued if anyone will, and I'll try not to let this
purgatory continue for a day longer than necessary.'

After that there was no possibility of establishing
a more friendly rapport. Judi took Dan's lead in
the continued efforts at survival because he seemed
to know what he was doing, but after all the tasks
were done they began to go their own ways. Judi
started to spend a lot of time in a half-moon cove
at the far end of the beach where she had first
opened her eyes to this nightmare, because it was
a place Dan rarely visited. She would sit for hours
gazing out to sea, willing a ship to appear over the
horizon, but none ever did.

When she began to realise the days were beginning to scramble into one seamless web she
started to keep a sort of tally, in age-old castaway
fashion, making a notch in a stick of wood each
morning, and, when she finished with one piece,
fixing it upright in the sand above the high-water
mark and starting on a second. They were small
pieces because they were easier to find and carry.

After three woods, as she called them, had gone
by, she began to look round for different ways of
keeping a track of things. After they had established an efficient routine of scavenging, fishing,
cooking and watching for ships, their days were
marked by few changes. But there were some things
she wanted to record forever. They were vignettes
in her mind, and she wanted to record them because they represented beauty and love and were
the small, precious things in life.

Like the time she had unexpectedly rounded a
bluff and found Dan waist-deep in the clear-as-

crystal water of a rock pool, his image glittering back from the unrippled surface as he stood as still as a piece of wind-carved rock himself. All at once she remembered a statue of a water god in the fountain at home, and her eyes filled with longing for all the old familiar places. The longing transferred itself automatically to Dan, for he was her home now. He was her salvation, whether she liked it or not, but above all he was where she yearned to belong.

She watched him for an age, knowing she would cherish the memory forever. There was a sort of loneliness in the pang of knowing she would never be able to share this feeling with anyone. Afterwards she pondered over the reasons for the strange hold he seemed to have over her. She knew it wasn't only because he put himself out of bounds. It was more than a longing for something she could never have.

She recognised with that part of herself that could be objective and businesslike that he had qualities that really did make him special. He was no ordinary man. Despite her feelings of hurt, she had to acknowledge this. It made her long to know more about him. He was, of course, a very handsome man, without physical flaw, a man any woman would want just by looking at him. The tough outdoor life enhanced his natural physical perfection, and now he was at his peak—mature, muscular, powerful, breath-stoppingly all-male. She would have had to be stone not to feel a primitive female response to him.

But it was more than just the way he looked that filled her with such an anguish of need. It was deeper than mere appearance. It was to do with character, she realised, the fact that whether he liked her or not he made her feel safe. She knew she could trust him. He would never let her down. Where other men were weak and indecisive, Dan was strong and single-minded. If he didn't know something he would try to work it out, assembling all the facts, analysing each separate part of the problem, restructuring it so that it made sense. Then, instead of simply leaving it there, he would put his theories into practice, taking immense care to get things right until, miraculously, everything worked. Like the spit system he had rigged up over the night-fire, like the hammock he had woven for her out of vines—going on to teach her how to make one herself. Like the fishing-nets he had constructed. And the idea of making sandals so that they could walk more comfortably over the rocks.

He was simply so clever and inventive, with a mind that was never still—Judi couldn't help loving him for it. It made him as engaging as a small boy as he puzzled over some fresh challenge to his ingenuity. This was the part of him she admired with her mind.

But there was yet another side to him, the side that really tugged her heart-strings, and it was an event in the cove that crystallised it for her, small though it was.

It was when she had discovered him standing in the coral cove, unaware of her presence, apparently watching for something. She had watched him, curious to know what he was up to. Then she had seen. He was calling the dolphins.

When she discovered this she would often steal over to the cove to watch, though something told her never to let him know. It was as if it was his secret place on the island, a place belonging to him alone, just as she had her moon cove. So she never told him she knew about it. But she would watch as he enticed the shy creatures to ever more daring feats of trust and courage.

Many times she had heard stories about how it was possible to communicate in some ways with these engaging creatures, but now she was able to witness the patience and sensitivity that were required in order to do so. Dan would stand for ages just waiting for them, and once they knew him and trusted him, come they would, swimming through a narrow gap in the reef at the mouth of the cove in a joyful surge, three or four at a time, and Dan would feed them titbits from his hand or play with them, tossing a hollow coconut back and forth like a ball, swimming alongside them, copying their movements and teaching them his.

It was this gentleness, an unexpected characteristic alongside the everyday toughness he displayed, that finally won her heart. There was something almost elemental in the acrobatic dance the creatures would weave around him, and it captivated her completely.

It became her favourite time of day, dolphin time, and just as she longed for Dan to show that same gentleness towards herself, so she longed for him to ask her to join them, but she knew he never would, because Kiss Doran was the last person to be invited to such a place.

         *   *   *

Inspired by his ingenuity, she resolved to solve a particular problem of her own, to do with keeping a record of events. In some ways she feared they would never be rescued, so, in her blackest mood, she wondered just what was the point of keeping a record with nobody to read it. But in more optimistic states of mind she knew it was worth doing for its own sake, and if they eventually got back home it would be a fascinating record. But how to do it?

She could have gone to Dan himself and asked his advice. For sure he would have come up with some sort of sensible suggestion, but they were scarcely talking to each other now. So she decided to solve the problem herself, eventually hitting on a strange concoction made from the sooty scrapings from the bottom of the kettle mixed with a gum from one of the unnamed species of plants. Paper was a problem, but less so, for there were numbers of leaves which dried to an oily texture firm enough to take the scratchings of a quill. It was simply a question of choosing the most favourable surface for her records.

If Dan observed these experiments, and she took a little care to keep them to herself in case they failed and she had to withstand his disparaging remarks, or, more likely, his advice, he said nothing. And Judi spent some time each evening writing down her observations and anything else that came to mind.

If there were only small makeshift changes day to day one thing that was changing rapidly was the weather.

So far it hadn't directly affected them, but for several days now the train of puffy white clouds that meant trade winds on the horizon had begun to cluster together in a darkening trail. Soon they spread over the whole sky, turning it grey, purpling to a dull, bruised look in the east.

'It looks as if we'll soon be having more water than we know what to do with,' Dan observed with his usual deadpan expression. He immediately set to solving the problem of storage tanks.

Judi began to remonstrate. She had been foraging for berries most of the day and her back ached abominably. The thought of having to set to on a task even more backbreaking was unthinkable. 'Surely we're not going to be here for much longer?' she demanded in scandalised tones. 'You can't really believe we need to conserve water for the months ahead?' Her face paled when she saw the confirmation in his eyes.

She went up to him and shook him by the arm. 'Why do you never tell me what's in your mind? I have a right to know!' She wanted to beat an answer from him, but his silence was as eloquent as words. 'It's true, isn't it? You don't think we'll ever get off the island, do you? You know we won't! We're here forever!' The thought appalled her.

Dan's face was blank. What did he feel? Did he feel anything?

She shook him by the arm. 'Tell me the truth, damn you! When you kept mentioning shipping lanes and keeping the beacon alight, you knew it was pointless, didn't you?'

She began to cry. His silence told her the worst. It unleashed a terrible fear, sending tears of devastating rage down her cheeks, though her face remained stark with shock.

She began to back away from him. 'Why didn't you tell me the truth? I should have guessed what you were thinking before now. Why didn't you tell me?' she demanded, her voice rising higher. 'I should have known, with all this effort——' She waved an arm around the neat camp with its by now many makeshift contraptions. 'Why else would you force me to go to all this trouble to make things? I imagined it was because it made life more comfortable for us both, because you liked fiddling about making things with your hands. But it wasn't that at all, was it? It's because you know we'll never escape.'

Still he didn't react.

'You've known all along!' she shouted, goaded by his lack of response. 'You've been fooling me—jollying me into accepting this living hell, making me think it was all going to be all right!' She took a deep breath. 'I hate you, Dan, you're a liar. You've been lying to me from day one! We're stuck here forever, aren't we? Forever! I can't bear it. *I hate you! I'd rather be dead!*'

Swivelling, her eyes blinded with the tears of fury that had suddenly forced themselves to the surface, she stumbled off towards the beach. She would rebuild the lifeboat with her bare hands, she would fill the holes with leaves if necessary, but she would get off this island if it was the last thing she did. Anything was better, she sobbed as her feet pounded across the sand, anything was better than being imprisoned here forever with a loathsome man who was as indifferent as a stone.

CHAPTER FOUR

DAN caught up with Judi before she was halfway across the beach. She felt his fingers dig deep into her shoulders, jerking her to a stop and sending her fists pummelling against his chest as she tried to free herself.

'Take your hands off me, Dan! I *hate* you!'

There was a crack of thunder as the storm drew near. His face was greyish in the eerie light that presaged the beginning. 'Listen to me, you little fool—we *shall* get away from here—I've already told you that. If it's humanly possible——'

'Sure, if it's *humanly* possible!' she yelled back, 'but you're not human, are you? Even though you seem to think so. And that's the answer to the question, isn't it? *If! If! If!* Well, it's *not* humanly possible, if you're the human! So I'm going to find a way to escape, and you can stay here and play at castaways till kingdom come!'

'Don't you think I *want* to escape?' His impassive look had given way to astonishment.

'You say you do, but I don't believe it. And I don't think you know how to do it any more than I do! In fact, I think you're actually *enjoying* all this—this horrible place, the squalor, the hideous things we have to eat, the insects, the—the——'

He was still gripping her tightly by the shoulders, and she could feel the tension in his fingertips as he tried to prevent her from escaping, but something happened, her words trailed away in confusion and she began to feel the fight draining out of her, but there was no way forward to what she desired, the only avenue was one of escape. With a flurried movement she ducked out of his grasp and ran towards the lifeboat. She didn't know what she was going to do, but it seemed to symbolise something deep inside that drove her on towards it.

She reached it before he did, and when he pounded up beside her she dodged, challenging him from the opposite side.

'*Leave me alone!* Let me do this my own way!' she shouted.

'Listen, Judi, I know it's rough and it may get worse,' Dan began, talking rapidly as if in an effort to control his feelings. 'I've been as honest as I can be with you. But I don't see the point of dwelling on the worst that might happen. That way we'd finish up suicidal—we'd turn in our tickets. Well, I'm not a quitter, and if that's what you want to do say so now. End it.'

'What do you mean?' She gazed at him in bewilderment.

'Just lie down and die,' he said harshly. 'That's your only alternative.'

'*You*...' Her teeth ground into her bottom lip, drawing blood. 'You hateful *monster*—you're utterly beyond words!'

'It's your choice,' he stated bluntly. 'I told you at the beginning, either we pull together or not at all.'

'There's no way we can pull together. We've proved that clearly enough. So it'll have to be not at all. But there isn't room enough on this island for both of us!'

'You're right. And *I'm* staying until I sight a rescue ship, so what are *you* going to do?'

She cast a fleeting glance at the lifeboat. It was totally unseaworthy, and she knew it. The coral reef had gouged out the bottom. Heaven alone knew how Dan had managed to get it ashore, with her unconscious body in it. 'I'll fix it,' she muttered through watering eyes. 'I'll do it somehow.'

'You're not setting out to sea in that.'

'Who says?'

'I do,' he said finally, turning to walk off.

'Is that so, Mr Super-Chief? Well, I've got news for you, and it's this.' She gripped the sides of the boat. '*I'll* fix it, don't you damn well worry. And then I'll be free. Free of this horrible place, and, best of all, free of *you*!'

He didn't even bother to turn round. He merely threw his head back and gave a deep, triumphant laugh.

'You'll laugh on the other side of your face!' she yelled impotently. '*I'll show you!*' She was trembling with rage and frustration. His broad back turned against her was salt in the wound, one more insult to add to all the rest.

He thinks I'm just a stupid, helpless, good-time type, all clawy fingernails and vanity, she thought as she began to heave at the side of the boat. He's never given me a chance to prove him wrong, because he's so damn sure he's always right.

She pushed at the side of the boat, hoping to turn it so she could inspect the damage more closely, though she knew he had made a thorough examination of it shortly after they had arrived. But it was massive, almost immovable, and she surveyed it in despair until she hit on the idea of wedging it with stones, rocking it till it tilted, then pushing more stones under it before it fell back into place. It was backbreaking work, slow and frustrating, because time after time the heavy weight dropped back before she could get the stones into position beneath it.

If only he'd help, she thought furiously, we could have it turned over in no time at all, then surely we could find a way of repairing it. She thought wildly of the next stage, of how to repair the ripped undersides, the thought that even Dan himself hadn't been able to solve the problem without the proper tools casting a gloom over the whole enterprise.

She worked until it was almost too dark to see, and even then she had only managed to get the boat tilted by about forty-five degrees, with hours of similar work ahead. She was shaking with exhaustion and anger by the time she trailed back up to base.

Dan didn't look up when she appeared, but there was something cooking in the pot, and she went over to give it a stir—after all, it was as much *her* pot and *her* fire, and probably food she herself had foraged for, as his, and she had a right to it. She dared him to warn her off. But he didn't. He seemed unaware of her presence.

She ladled a helping into the shell of a coconut— *her* work, she remembered, scooping out the white flesh, then holding up the empty shell with a triumphant, 'Soup bowl!' then later gathering more

and teaching herself how to open them so that they
formed a sufficient hollow to contain a helping of
broth. Without me he'd still be eating out of the
kettle, she thought, squatting on the ground beside
the fire. He had never acknowledged any of the
little things she'd done to make life more bearable.

The fire began to hiss, and she looked up in
alarm. It was raining. Large, separate drops fell,
with spaces between. It stopped as suddenly as it
started, and she wondered if the promised deluge
to solve their water problems was wishful thinking
after all.

Exhausted, she lay down in her hammock with
the intention of getting some sleep so she could
make an early start next morning. But something
jerking at the strings of the hammock nearly pitched
her out on to the ground. She clung on and raised
her head.

'What are you doing that for?' she demanded.
Dan was gripping the twine that attached the
hammock to a tree.

'Get up. The rain's coming. We have things to
do.'

'Go to *hell*!' Judi lay back in the hammock and
shut her eyes.

'Judi, get up, will you!'

Keeping her eyes shut, she muttered, 'Go away—
I'm tired.'

'I don't care whether you're tired or ready to
disco all night, I'm telling you to get out. I need
another pair of hands.'

'*Tough!*' she retorted, casting a quick glance at
him out of the corners of her eyes. She could only
see his shape outlined against a purple sky. The

tropical storm was almost upon them, approaching
with an air of lingering menace.

'I'll ask you one more time.'

'*Ask?*' She sat up. 'I was under the impression
you only gave orders.'

Dan sighed. 'Are you going to help or not?'

'No, actually,' she said with exaggerated
boredom, 'I don't believe I am.'

'We'll see about that.' He turned and marched
to the tree-trunk from which the hammock was
suspended and proceeded to untie the knot that held
it.

'You oaf!' Before it fell to the ground Judi
scrambled out, standing furiously with the folds
cascading around her ankles. Dan gave a soft laugh
to add to her humiliation.

'*Now* will you do as I say?'

'Why the hell should I?' she shouted at the top
of her voice, in vain trying to untangle her feet from
the net.

'Because,' he answered in a quiet voice as if to
underline her lack of control, 'in a few short moments we'll have more water from heaven than we
know what to do with. I intend to catch some of
it for the dry days ahead, as I have a vested interest
in getting out of this place alive. If you'll pause
and give the matter a moment's rational thought—
assuming you're capable of such a thing—you'll
realise we can't afford not to do as I say.'

'Really? I will, will I?' She kicked the last of the
net aside.

'Well?' He gave an impatient jerk of his head.
'Are you coming to help or not?'

Without even bothering to reply Judi walked towards him. He turned, already knowing she would follow. For what else could she do? she thought furiously. If he had some plan in his head it was bound to be right, wasn't it? He was Superman, wasn't he? Never putting a foot wrong. At least as far as the boring practical details went . . . in *human* terms he hadn't even entered the contest. She was full of bitterness. He closed all avenues, putting her in the wrong from morning to night.

He stalked on ahead of her, finally fetching up on the beach again, and when he reached the lifeboat, so laboriously tilted on to its side that afternoon, Judi opened her mouth in astonishment. Then she let out a cry when she saw what he was going to do.

Springing forward, she put out her hands to stop him. 'You *can't*! It took me hours to turn it——'

'Sorry, you should have liaised with me before putting so much effort into it. I warned you we had to work together.'

'*Together?* Your idea of together is for you to give the orders and for me to obey them!'

'Until you come up with a few sound ideas of your own—yes, that's exactly what it comes down to. Ready?'

She gazed at him in horror. Why hadn't he warned her what was in his mind? All that work, that effort, all for nothing. Her hands were sore, full of splinters. Her back ached, and she was close to tears.

'I said, ready?'

She avoided his glance. 'What do you want me to do?'

'Heave when I say heave. I want it turned back again. You're going to have to put all your strength into it. I'm going to line it with that piece of polythene we've got, then we can catch enough water in it for all our foreseeable needs. Ready?'

Together they rocked the boat back and forth, until with a grunt Dan gave the signal to push it over. As it landed with a crash on the sand Judi stepped back, her heart like lead as she saw her hours of hard work undone in a few seconds. Why hadn't she fought him over it? she asked herself. She could have insisted that she was going to put to sea in it, couldn't she? Now her chance was gone for good.

I hate you, Dan, she thought silently, turning away. Raindrops were beginning to hiss all around them, kicking up the sand like bullets, and soon the rain was forming rivulets down the beach, gouging out channels as it ran back into the sea.

Dan was already sprinting towards camp, and she saw him return with their precious piece of polythene, the one that had been set up as a solar still. She had no idea whether he'd worked out how to keep it in place in the bottom of the boat, but she took it for granted he had already got some scheme in mind.

She made her way towards the fire, feeling defeated and useless. When she got back she gazed in consternation as a few weak flames fluttered in a sea of ash. In another few minutes the rain would have put it out completely. Why hadn't they thought of that? If the beacon went out too they had only another carefully conserved couple of matches with which to light it again.

Looking wildly round for some way of saving the last of the flames, she picked up the nearest thing to hand and gently scooped up the few branches that were still alight, carrying them carefully in a coconut shell to the shelter of the rocks. At midday it was a place where there was always some shadow and it would provide some shelter now. She put the lighted brands inside a fissure and heaped dry kindling around them, coaxing them back to life and sighing with relief when the flames brightened and began to lick greedily at the fuel she was putting on.

Then she remembered the tarpaulin Dan had rigged up as a wind-break when they first arrived, and leaving the fire for a minute she ran across the clearing and ripped it from its supports to drag it across to the rocks where the fire was burning. Somehow she contrived to weight the two corners with boulders and with the help of a couple of branches from the woodpile propped it tent-style over the fire. There was just room to crawl underneath, and she was there, anxiously tending the flames, when Dan came back.

She heard him call out, then the edge of the tarpaulin lifted. The space beneath was full of smoke, and he coughed as it swirled towards him. 'Room for two under there?' Without waiting for an answer he crawled in beside her out of the rain. His skin was a glistening honey-brown, black hair, longer by now, slicked close to his scalp. He rubbed it with both hands, scattering drops of rain over Judi's bare legs, then leaned in towards the warmth of the flames to dry it.

'We'll have to go outside and bring in a stack of wood,' he observed. 'Keep enough of it dry to last as long as we need. Then make sure we keep ourselves dry too. It'd be disastrous if we get pneumonia on top of everything else.'

No thanks, no praise—well, so what's new? thought Judi, noting his impassive face. Nothing, not even this latest turn of events, got through to him. She had just been shouting out her lungs, screaming into his face that she hated him, but what reaction was there? Nothing.

'Yes,' she said, getting up, 'I'll go and drag some more in before it gets thoroughly soaked.'

Already the rain was thrumming on the tarpaulin as if it would never stop, but the fire, after its near demise, was now blazing cheerily, drying out the space between the walls of rock and creating a welcome fug.

She dipped her head and plunged out into the deluge, surprised to find Dan following her. Together they dragged the best of the wood back, thrusting it quickly under cover, then, as she turned to fetch the cooking things, Dan followed her, obviously with the same idea in mind.

Puffing and panting, she looked up at the same moment and their eyes met. He gave a sudden grin. It was such a dazzle, full of spontaneous warmth, that Judi stopped dead in her tracks and simply gaped at him with the rain pelting down and running in rivulets down their faces.

'What's up?' he asked, eyebrows rising. The grin was replaced by his usual guarded expression, and she dropped her glance at once.

'Nothing.' She shook her head and bent to pick up some more wood. Dan did likewise.

But they were working as a team and they both knew it. His on-off smile had signalled the fact. That was what it had meant. At least, she thought to herself, I'm doing something right for once, even though he hasn't exactly said so in words.

Together they transferred everything to the makeshift shelter and were soon settled back inside.

'This rain has really caught me on the hop,' he began. 'It seems to have arrived sooner than I'd calculated.' He busied himself with the freshly filled kettle, an absorbed expression on his face as if he was concentrating on the task in hand. 'According to the records,' he went on, 'it shouldn't arrive until the end of the month.'

'Which month?' she asked.

'The one after the one in which we arrived.' He turned away.

'I think it probably has,' she said. She was scraping with the one knife they possessed at some breadfruit, thinking it would be comforting to eat something while they sat out the bad weather.

'Probably has what?' he asked, not looking up.

'Come at the end of the month after we arrived.'

'No. We're not more than twelve to fifteen days into it.'

Judi was silent. She had the five woods to prove he was wrong, but she wasn't interested in scoring points. The rain was here on schedule, but so what? It would have been as wet and welcome whether early or late. She sighed and went on scraping.

Dan put the lid on the kettle and crouched beside her. 'What's that expression on your face supposed to mean? Have I said something wrong again?'

She glanced up. 'It doesn't matter.'

He took the knife from between her fingers. 'And if I say it does?'

Judi could feel his fingers holding hers. The air inside the shelter was stifling. There was a smell of smoke and cooking and under it the musky tang of their two bodies, rain-wet skin, male and female, Dan's as familiar as her own, and arousing a tenderness she didn't want to feel. She looked anywhere but into his eyes, feeling more naked than she had ever felt before.

'Judi?' His voice was a husky growl beneath the drumming overhead.

'It doesn't matter,' she whispered.

He let her fingers go and turned his head, saying conversationally, 'I meant to keep a record of the phases of the moon as a sort of calendar, but I thought we were going to be picked up fairly soon, and by the time I realised we were in for a long stay I'd lost count of the time that had elapsed. I suppose time is something you intuitively know about.' He turned to look at her.

She flushed and gave a small shrug and tried to avoid his glance. She knew what he meant. Knowing how her femininity seemed to irritate him, she had taken care not to betray the detailed personal matters that took place. It had been difficult, but she had coped. She said, 'I've been keeping a double check, actually. It seemed a good idea in case we were here for a long time to keep a tally of the days. We're at the end of the second month now. Your rains must be bang on schedule.'

He said, 'Oh,' and looked thoughtful. He was still crouching beside her. There was so little room that they couldn't manage a more comfortable distance between them. Not now. But Judi felt as if his presence was a deliberate encroachment, filling the whole space, swamping her, and she wanted to get away before she started to tell him all about her wood calendar and the secret cove, but there was nowhere to go, and she fought to remain silent. It was no good telling him stuff like that, she told herself, because a confession about the cove would only lead to her betrayal of the fact that she knew about his dolphins, and then she would have to bear the brunt of some cutting remark or other, a warning to keep away—and her picture of paradise would be denied her forever.

Instead she bent her head to her task again, and when she had finished she put the breadfruit in the kettle and waited for them to cook. Dan sat beside her and seemed to be counting the drops of water as they slid down the side of the rock behind the fire. For once he wasn't busy with something, and she realised how strange it was to see him sitting idly without some piece of work in his hands. But there was a familiar look on his face and she guessed he was busy working something out, calculating some useful formula, the cubic capacity of the lifeboat and likely number of litres they would use per day, perhaps. She gave a half-smile just as he turned to her.

His blue eyes dilated, darkening with interrogation. Before he could put the question into words she told him what she had been thinking, half believing she had really picked up what had been in his mind. He gave a short laugh. 'So you think my thoughts dwell exclusively on technical matters, do you?' He put a finger out and stopped a drip of water above her head. 'You must find that quite difficult to live with.'

'It doesn't matter,' she said in a repetition of the words she had used a few moments ago. 'It's quite interesting.'

He looked at her for a moment as if making up his mind whether to say something or not, then he said, 'Apart from one or two understandable flare-ups you've hardly complained about anything. You're not the whingeing type. This would be a hundred times worse if you were. Thank you for that.'

'There's no point in whingeing, is there? We're here whether we like it or not. We have to get on with it.'

'That's what I mean. A lot of women would find something to complain about in a five-star hotel. You, in this God-forsaken spot, don't make a murmur.' Dan reached out and took her hand, turning it over and looking at the weals that had come up after struggling with the boat. She felt her nerves begin to quiver with expectation. He had never touched her like this before. Suddenly the air seemed charged with mystery. With a brief movement of his head he pressed a kiss into her palm. There she assumed it was meant to end. He had been touched for a moment by the sight of her work-scarred hands, guilt, perhaps, forcing him to a moment's contrition. But at the moment of contact everything changed.

It was the signal for something to release itself. With a muffled groan he enveloped her in his arms, and with a gasp she found her lips lifting, seeking his as they came searching for hers with the same intention. Her body seemed to sing, tingling with the long-repressed need to touch and be touched, her naked breasts tightening in a spasm of pleasure as his rough chest scoured her with the urgency of desire.

Somehow he was lying over her as she found herself stretched full length beneath him, his arousal evident as he pressed against her. She felt her mouth open, drinking him in as his tongue searched out some deep well of yearning. Their limbs moved in a fevered dance, exploring each other in every variety of sensual touch, light and strong, rough to the point of pain, delicate with the finest nuance of physical contact. In the half-light she could see his face above her own, and now for the first time she saw that the familiar guarded look had gone. Instead it was suffused with light. His eyes were burning through the darkness, eating her up. There was nothing impersonal in that look at all. It said he wanted to be with no other woman but her. His husky words confirmed it.

'I want you, Judi,' he groaned. 'I want you so much. But if you tell me not to go on, I won't if you don't want me too.'

Her eyes drank in the abrupt transformation and she gazed up into his beloved face as he held himself in a state of tension above her with a look reflecting his unhidden desire. How had she hated

this man only hours ago? she asked herself. It was
because she loved him that she had hated him so
fiercely. Even though she didn't know what had led
him to open the shutters to her now, how could she
deny him when he was all her world?

'Tell me, Judi...I'll stop if you want me to...'
he insisted in a voice hoarse with desire.

'No...don't stop!' She pulled his head down
more fiercely, seeking his mouth and giving him
her tongue with a feeling that nothing else mattered
but this moment, this giving, this loving, as if the
life outside their tiny space no longer existed.
'Please make love with me,' she whispered. 'I want
you, Dan.' I want you forever...she added silently.
Forever.

With a gasp of surprise he hardened against her,
and then she felt him quicken, taking her power-
fully into his embrace, sweeping her up into his
world with an irresistible strength that transported
her beyond any bounds she had ever known.

Outside their den the thunder began to roll. The
storm seemed to go on without end, lightning
ripping the heavens apart, the clouds distending to
let down the beneficence of their contents. Dan's
lovemaking seemed to be part of the storm itself,
steam and rain and the heat of their two bodies
melding in a vapour that was elemental, earth, air,
water and above all, fire.

'I shall remember this night forever,' Judi whispered as the sky turned lavender with flame, losing
his reply as the heavens ripped open again and
again. 'I shall love you forever, Dan, my darling
Dan,' she murmured, her words losing themselves

in the thunder-cracks overhead. 'I knew love could be extraordinary. I knew it could be like this.'

Later she said, 'When they tried to marry me off to someone I didn't love, I had to run away. I knew it was right to leave, to come and find you. I knew you were waiting for me...'

She let him love her as much as he wanted, for there was nothing ahead but love. It was here now in her arms. On a night like this there could only be love.

CHAPTER FIVE

WHEN Judi opened her eyes it was to find everything bathed in a surreal green light. It was like being under water. The rain roaring on the tarpaulin added to the effect. Her left side felt crushed, and she saw it was because Dan was lying against her, one arm held tightly around her waist. Then she recalled the events of the night with a rush of tenderness. Without waking him she began to extricate herself from his embrace, then lay for a long time just looking at his sleeping form in the strange green filtered light.

Everything that had happened seemed unreal. Snatches of half-heard phrases that the thunder hadn't quite been able to drown out in the night floated back to her—Dan's love talk, his wanting, needing, desiring her, always now, wanting now, loving now, and her own words matching his, whispering only of the present, now, please...their voices merging...now, his demands made in that husky, thrilling voice she could not resist. It had been as if the future could never touch them, as if they were castaways not only in space but in time as well. They were in a rainbow-hued bubble, a time-capsule, separated from the rest of the universe forever, outside its laws and expectations.

Very soon he began to wake up, and she watched the changes in his face as sleep drained away from him, then he opened his eyes. They homed straight

into her own as if he had been seeking her even in
his dreams. They were bright and blue and full of
love. He took her back into his arms at once,
fondling her with his strong, sensitive hands,
making nothing of any lingering doubts she might
have had that it had all been some kind of storm-
driven dream, two people driven together by a
mutual sense of their own mortality beneath the
mighty hand of nature. It wasn't that—she could
see it in his eyes. It was love, mirroring her own.

'I'll keep you safe,' he vowed, as if reading her
mind. 'We're going to survive. Together we can see
it through.' His kisses banished every fear, and
somewhere deep in her heart she knew it was real,
as real as the promises he had made in the night.
She thought, if it's my fate to die at this moment,
my life will be complete. Everything is perfect now.
There's nothing more to desire. I have it all here in
my arms. My love. And my love loves me. Her eyes
were shining as she lifted her lips to his.

Much later they managed to drag themselves
from their warm nest and brave the still torrential
rain. All morning it had been thundering on the
tarpaulin and dripping in great heavy drops down
the side of the rock, but they had been able to cling
together for warmth, and it was only necessity that
forced them out at last. They ran hand in hand
down the beach to plunge headlong into the wild
surf where it flung its frothing curtains of billowing
lace against the shore. It was dazzling and spine-
tingling and tried to pull their sleek bronze bodies
into its treacherous realm, but Dan kept a tight hold
of Judi's hand and warned her against going in too
far, and when the snaking arms of Neptune took

a grip on her he held her safe within his own embrace, the fingers of the surf powerless against his greater strength. He was her rock, her saviour, and she lifted up her arms to let them slide around his neck.

'I've never loved anyone like this before,' she told him, passion in her upturned face. 'I didn't know I would want to feel so weak in a man's arms! But I do! And I don't care!'

'Weak? My angel weak?' Dan's blue eyes danced. 'You're as strong as nature. You're earth woman. You're the first woman of creation. Mother earth.' Later he called her moon goddess when the storm abated, and between the ragged clouds the falcate moon began to walk its ancient path, mysterious with hidden power. It seemed infinitely strange to them as they looked up at it on their small island in the middle of the vast space of the ocean. 'She commands all the tides and ourselves with her invisible force,' he murmured. 'It's like love, pervading every living thing.'

'It's like being Adam and Eve,' said Judi, 'loving each other in the first Garden of Creation.' She sighed. 'Do you think they looked up at the moon like us and wondered about its power and what drew them together with such a sense of destiny?'

'I think Eve was never loved like this,' Dan told her, taking her into his arms. 'This is the first real love affair in the history of the world.'

'Affair?' She raised her head.

'Event—a love event. The one which all others follow, pale shadows of the real thing.'

'You don't talk like a sailor,' she murmured. 'Or do you? Are they romantics at heart like you? I do love you, Dan,' she repeated, knowing the words didn't express the fullness of what was in her heart. 'I've never met a man like you before. You're strong and sensitive, tough and gentle. You're everything—all things. You're the most mysterious being I've ever encountered. I think you must be from another planet.'

'And you're Venus,' he told her, 'from the planet of love.'

'Then,' she said, remembering a painting from a distant time and place, 'you must be Mars, god of thunder, war, and men.' She gave a quirky smile. 'I've always fought to be equal, but I'm giving it up bit by bit. I feel as if I belong to you now, Dan. You're my strength. It's a strange feeling—scary, as if you possess me. It's never happened before, and I've never wanted it to happen before. I've always been my own woman, taking orders from no one.' She gave a shiver. She understood all of a sudden how much he could hurt her.

He turned away, missing the change of expression on her face. 'Before we met is another time. It doesn't seem to matter now. We've broken with the past. Whatever was in that world might as well never have existed.'

'Whatever happened,' she agreed, 'it was nothing, of no account. I can scarcely imagine that world!' She took his arm and made him turn to face her. 'You think we'll never go back there, don't you?'

'Will you shout at me again if I say I have my doubts?'

She shook her head. 'I only shouted because I thought you didn't like me.'

Dan ruffled her hair. 'I didn't like you, though I did desire you.' When she pretended to pull a face he added quickly, 'I didn't like what the world seemed to have made you—that affected behaviour, your superficial values, that terrible make-up.'

'You glimpsed me once in a most uncharacteristic situation!' she exclaimed, defending herself with a laugh. 'Honestly, I wasn't really as bad as you thought I was! And,' she teased, 'it's very unkind to judge me on such a brief encounter!'

'You reminded me of too many other women,' he said seriously. 'I get impatient with that type.' His eyes were watchful.

'I'm not that type.'

'No. In this place, in this time, in this place out of time...' His voice thickened. 'In paradise, my angel, you are the only woman...I've forgotten the rest of the world, it no longer exists. You are all there is and all I desire.'

Judi's eyes were suddenly watchful. 'Oh, my love,' she bit her lip, knowing that her heart was thumping with a sudden fear, 'do you mean you might feel differently, back in the outside world?'

He pulled her roughly into his arms without speaking. She could feel his lips pressuring over her forehead and she tilted her head back and felt them linger over her face, finding her lips, taking them, exerting the familiar magic again before she pulled even further back, her eyes full of questions.

'Can you believe there could ever be anyone else for me after this?' he demanded in husky tones. 'Can't you see how crazy I am about you? Don't you trust what we have now?'

'I'd die without you,' she whispered.

'That's not an answer.' His jaw, almost concealed beneath the growth of black beard that defied the daily barbering with the scissor-attachment of his knife, tightened a fraction, telling her how important her answer was to him.

For a brief second she paused. The outside world was impossible to envisage. How could she not trust his love now that he was everything to her? They were all there was for each other, would be so, forever. It could never be otherwise. She took him in her arms. 'Love, my love,' she whispered. 'I love you and trust you. We live in paradise, and there's no other world but this...'

She knew it wasn't quite the wholehearted affirmation of trust he seemed to demand, but how could she say she would trust him in the outside world when she didn't know who he was in that world? There he would be a stranger to her and she to him. She knew there must be things about the past that neither of them had confessed yet.

Only in the beauty of the moon-shaped cove where they made love was there no room for doubt.

By the time the storm ceased the lifeboat was brimming with water. 'Enough to last for some time,' observed Dan.

'But then what?' asked Judi. She smiled. 'We won't worry. I feel things are going to be different from now on.'

She began to plan a garden, a place where she could cultivate the edible plants they had found and perhaps, if she kept them properly weeded and cared for, they'd grow bigger and be more nu-

tritious. She was also planning a clay oven of some
sort. But that would need discussion, as she wasn't
quite sure how to set about it. The rain had churned
up what little soil there was, and now it was baking
hard again in the sun.

Later that day she put the idea to Dan, and they
set about devising a way of carting the mud to where
they could build it into the structure they wanted.
He thought it an excellent idea, and said so. Judi
beamed.

She had never felt so content in her life. Her
fingernails no longer mattered. Even her hair, the
perfect bob, had grown out and hung in dark ten-
drils around her face in a way it hadn't done since
childhood. Dan said it suited her. He twined flowers
in it and called her his earth goddess again. They
stopped wearing clothes completely, all need for
them a thing of the past, but with the sudden
blossoming of the vegetation that had lain dormant
in the dry season they decorated each other and
brought rare specimens from other parts of the
island to show each other.

Once Dan handed her a showy scarlet flower, and
she took it with a smile of delight, but dropped it
with a cry as a grotesque horned insect crawled out
of it and flew off. It reminded her of a poem about
a rose with something dark at its heart, and she felt
a momentary foreboding, and realised she was becoming superstitious. She had missed greeting the
new moon recently, and the omission weighed on
her as if she had stored up retribution for herself.

When she told Dan he laughed and kissed her
fondly on the nape of the neck. 'You are funny—

so practical and strong in some things and just crazy in others.'

She teased him in turn about his dolphin friends, for by now he knew she had discovered his secret, and she wouldn't let him forget how he had told her in complete seriousness that they were beginning to understand certain words. Now she went to the cove with him, and sometimes it seemed as if he was right.

'They're like children,' she said thoughtfully as the dolphins came at his call. She felt pleased that he was so gentle and understanding with them, and such fun too. Children needed that.

They inspected the woods in Judi's cove—the moon cove, Dan called it. He said he knew she worshipped the moon in secret there because that was the only way she could have such power over him. He was in thrall to her, her devoted acolyte. He made love to her in the crescent cove by the light of the moon to show her what he meant.

'You're all silvery,' she told him, storing up this image along with all the rest.

The woods were many now. Nearly half a year, Judi said, counting.

'We were blown well off course in that freak event... It all seems so long ago.' Dan looked puzzled. 'I would have thought...' he stopped. 'Perhaps we'll light up the beacon again. We've become very lax.'

'Fire?' she asked.

'I'll solve that one.' It had gone out long ago. 'It can be done.'

Sure enough, he made fire once more after many unsuccessful attempts. The frail smoke rose into the

air like a tiny triumph of nature. Now they felt they
were working with nature and not fighting her. They
sat by the glinting fire-beacon until the sun went
down, drowsing in each other's arms, too
comfortable to move. There was nothing to stop
them making love anywhere they liked. They possessed the whole island, and made it a temple to
love.

Life became an idyll, a paean to love, and it
seemed that every drowsing moment was as full with
the richness of life as it could ever be. Somehow
there was no time for all the questions that could
have been asked when they first met—the sort of
questions any two strangers on the brink of becoming lovers might ask. They seemed to live in a
continuous present, for the past was irretrievable
and a future anywhere but here a practical
impossibility.

Despite this, intimations of other times and other
places cast a flimsy shadow over the present now
and then and one or other of them would raise their
glance, blue eyes would open a fraction as if to en-
compass some new fact.

Sometimes, sitting alone in her moon cove, Judi
would dream about Dan's life before they met,
would carefully arrange the words in preparation
for a question when she next had the opportunity,
but somehow, in the somnolent weeks after the
storm, when the island itself seemed to be dreamily
ripe with new life, there was neither the time nor
the inclination to introduce matters that were no
longer relevant and the questions would go un-
asked, the moment would become golden again,
weaving itself invisibly into the fabric of their days.

Dan himself must also have felt curiosity, she realised, but if he did he seemed to be in thrall to the same indolent gods, for he asked nothing about her life in 'the other world', as they called it, except for the barest details, even though Judi did get around to mentioning Patrick again. 'My reason for running away from home,' she explained sleepily one afternoon down on the beach in Moon Cove. 'They tried to tell me I was going to marry him. I said no, I shan't! and ran away to be a DJ on a ship.'

The cruise liner seemed like a fragment from a half-forgotten dream.

'Chance, then, that you finished up on my ship,' Dan murmured, trailing sand grains over her bare arm in little whorls, following some intricate design of his own.

She pressed her lips against his shoulder as he leaned over her. 'Finished?' she asked drowsily. 'I didn't finish up on it, my love, but off it! Here with you. Chance—beautiful chance.'

'Life.' His handsome, enigmatic face softened as his eyes met hers. 'We owe our lives to chance, to fortune. Our lives, our love.'

He was never cold now. His eyes were never that arctic blue as they once had been, but were always now dawn-blue, soft as sky, his lips gentle except in the deep extremes of passion, and never tight with impatience or derision as they once had been. Love had softened his aggression. He spent time in idleness too, though the jobs still got done, and the invention of some new gadget was never far out of his mind.

She avoided asking him why he had been so hostile to begin with for fear it would unlock things that would spoil the idyll of the present. Those early days were like a bad dream, but one that had miraculously turned good. She didn't want to revive memories of how it had been.

Looking at him now, with his black beard and rakishly long hair that together with a dark tan and flashing smile made him look like a gypsy or a pirate king, she could hardly remember the time when his face had been hard and cold and his indifference towards her had seemed total. Now he would chase her along the beach and when he caught her would envelop her in a bear-like hug, carrying her giggling and squirming down to the water's edge.

His rough kisses made her feel protected from all dangers, and although she knew he could hurt her in other more subtle ways she was beginning to feel he never would.

She loved to bask in his embrace with the water lapping around them, tasting the salt on his skin, breathing in the scent of the ocean on it. They played together like children, carelessly, inventing games of makebelieve that might go on all day and into the night, or they would spend hours grooming each other, plaiting each other's hair, the first time, Judi reaching out in wonderment to touch Dan's lips with her fingertips, stunned by how handsome he looked with his hawklike profile, her eyes moistening with a sudden sense of time passing and the fragility of life.

'You're beautiful too,' he breathed, misunderstanding the mistiness in her eyes and covering her face with soft, exploratory kisses. He wove flowers in her hair, mixing reds and violets in the dark locks like a crown, then called her his goddess, and then they were like children, pretending to be somewhere else and not themselves, changing everything. Except of course for love—which remained unchanged.

Sometimes Judi caught a shadow of an emotion she couldn't name that came over his face sometimes without warning. Shaking him, she would ask, 'What is it, love?' but he would smile again, his eyes softening, and he would grip her fiercely against him, crushing the breath from her body in a fierce spasm of desire, and invariably they would make love, and she would worship his passion and his tenderness, marvelling that the cold, hostile man who had arrived on the island with her had been transformed by its magic power into a lover of consummate sensitivity.

'My gentle dolphin man!' she joked tenderly. 'You play with those creatures as if they're your little children.' Turning away to pick a flower, she didn't see the blue turn to petrel, stormy, dark and troubled, as his eyes hungrily explored her naked form while she knelt in the grass.

Some things they did learn about each other, but in an episodic sort of way, little facts leaking from the other world into the present. Judi learned how Dan had gone to school in New York, captained at football and baseball, and she told him about her own school and tennis and netball. It led them to mark out a pitch on which to play a hybrid invention, part baseball, part cricket, which usually ended in a laughing dispute over suddenly invented 'rules' by whoever was losing at the time, and, like almost everything, the conclusion was only reached when they found each other's arms and love took over.

Dan confessed to being a solitary child outside school—mainly, he said, without elaboration, for family reasons. Judi tried to imagine the school in a world she didn't know, the solitary boy, the poor family that made it difficult to invite friends back, for she could think of no other reason for her handsome Dan to be other than gregarious by nature. When he mentioned an ailing mother the picture was complete. She cuddled him to make up for all the fun he'd missed and carefully told him about her own rambling family, deliberately not dwelling too much on the fact that they were, had always been, wealthy and privileged, and how her own childhood had been full of light and laughter and wishes come true.

Dwelling on this, in the solitude of Moon Cove, she began to see how she had always had what she wanted, and it came as an unpleasant thought that perhaps she had been rather spoiled, hence those first difficult episodes with Dan. Used as he was to having to fight for anything he wanted, it was natural he hadn't taken kindly to what must have seemed to him her high-handed manner. It all seemed clear to her now, and she smiled to herself at the mystery solved.

She was just too used to getting her own way, and he was too used to *having* to get his . . . in order to survive.

CHAPTER SIX

JUDI rubbed her eyes. She had been staring out to sea for some time, her eyes seemingly fixed of their own volition on something, until at last she had had to focus on what they were telling her and make sense of it. 'It's a dream. It must be!' she whispered.

There was neither joy nor fear in her heart as she stared at the apparition sailing towards the island. Then suddenly a cry was ripped from her throat. *'Dan!'* she shrieked, spinning on her heel and tearing off at top speed down the side of the hill. 'Dan! Dan—it's a ship! Quickly—look!' When she found him she was breathless, almost incoherent with the news. 'I don't believe my eyes!' she cried, grabbing him by the arm and forcing him to run with her towards the beach. 'Look, look—can you see it? Is it *real*?'

She had turned and turned again as she ran to find him, sure she would lose sight of the ship and it would disappear forever, as if by keeping it in her line of vision she could control its presence.

But now Dan could see it too. He said nothing at first, but there was a stunned look on his face. 'It's making for the island,' he said at last. 'Get up on to the hill, pile more wood on to the beacon in case they haven't seen it. Quickly, hurry! I've got to get the glass.' He had a reflecting glass, kept in a safe place for as long as she could remember. Now he ran to find it.

LOVE ISLAND

Perhaps he knows Morse too, Judi thought as she ran in a fever of anticipation to the top of the hill with her arms bundled up with fuel. She threw it on the fire and nearly scorched herself with the fierce blaze that got up. 'Oh help, God, please don't let it sail on by. Please let them see us!' *People,* she thought, *the outside world. I'm frightened.*

In an hour the ship was standing off in the bay. It seemed enormous, a noisy, turbulent monster, dwarfing the horizon.

'It's an oil tanker,' Dan told her. 'Watch, they're sending out a lighter.'

She saw a small boat separate itself from the mother ship and bob across the blue sea towards them. There were some men in it in uniform. The wake of the boat was as white as snow behind it.

Judi slipped her hand in Dan's. 'It's taking ages to get here,' she said. Even now it seemed as if the little boat might turn back and abandon them in paradise.

'The current's strong out there,' he told her. Then he glanced down at her, his eyes crinkling fondly. 'If you don't want to shock them you'd better try to find something to cover yourself with!'

She glanced down at her innocent body with wide eyes. 'Heavens, I'd forgotten clothes! What a scandal! But what can I put on?'

He threw his head back with a laugh. 'Not a woman in the world but she says, "I haven't a thing to wear"!'

'Well, I haven't!' she giggled, and he gripped her in a convulsive hug that took her breath away.

'I love you, Judi. But hurry—I want us to meet them together.'

Dan wore the remnants of a pair of shorts, made of more substantial material than the flimsy cocktail dress of long ago which had been Judi's only attire the night of the disaster, but she had kept it, some sequins still clinging to the fabric even now, and wrapped it as best she could sarong-style to cover the parts she wanted only Dan to see, then she hurried back to the beach. She was in time to see the boat come riding high on a mountain of surf through the reef.

When at last it beached Dan strode straight down to it, and, drawing back a little, Judi waited until the explanations seemed to be over before shyly stepping forward. The men seemed to be talking too loudly, too fast, too much. Their gestures seemed crude, their bodies overweight and un-healthy. They stood round Dan in a rough semi-circle, listening to what he had to say and pointing back at the ship. It made her want to retreat to the furthest corner of their home, to let these strangers go on their way again. They were an intrusion in paradise. They were here to rip her world apart.

But Dan turned with a smile as she came down to them. 'This is a great day, Judi. It's an American ship. They're taking us back home!'

Once the men had agreed to take them back to the ship there was nothing to delay their departure. 'There's nothing to pack, nothing to take.' Dan glanced back once towards the camp. 'We have nothing of value.'

Judi pulled her hand out of his. An anguish shot through her as if he had said something deliberately wounding. 'Hadn't we better—I mean, shouldn't we put out the fire at least and——' Her bottom lip trembled.

'Idiot—it's hardly going to cause any damage! It'll go out by itself.' Dan was already halfway to the boat. 'Come on! What's the matter?' His whole body was taut with the prospect of departure. Ordinarily his excitement would have been contagious, but this time something held Judi back from sharing in it.

'But, Dan——' She couldn't explain. They were walking out on their home. How could he do it without a backward glance? And how could he say they had nothing of value? Her eyes glistened.

He strode back to where she stood and took her forcibly by the arm. 'Don't worry, they'll find some clothes for you as soon as we get on board. They're broad-minded chaps, but not animals. You'll be quite safe.'

He had misunderstood her reluctance to leave. With her head bent she allowed him to run her to the water's edge, where the crewmen, impatient to get back, were already climbing on board. The boat lifted and fell on the crests of the breaking waves, and they were all drenched by the time they began to force their way through the gap in the reef.

On the way across the bay Dan talked exclusively to the men, describing how he had managed to steer them to safety through the reef so long ago, and how they had barely managed to keep going without water, without anything other than the short-term survival gear from the lifeboat.

As he talked the island, at first large and dominant, became progressively smaller, until by the time they were climbing the ladder on to the vast tanker it was an insignificant dot in the endless panorama of ocean and sky.

How can it look so unimportant? Judi wondered. It was our whole world for all our lifetime together.

By now wrapped modestly in a ship's blanket, she slipped her hand into Dan's as they were led up and down stairways and along corridors in the bowels of the iron ship. It was bigger than their entire island. She was lost already.

Led to the captain's quarters, they separated immediately to have showers and clothes found for them. The captain's wife helped Judi into a blouse and skirt. The material felt uncomfortable against her skin and she chafed at the restrictions of buttons and zips, and later, when nobody was looking, she slipped off the pair of sandals that had been found for her and left them under a table. Pleading a tiredness she didn't feel, she went to lie down in the cabin that had been prepared for her and wondered what Dan was doing. He seemed to have been absorbed at once into the masculine world of ships and ship's officers. She missed him already. They had been apart for at least two hours.

It was the first separation in seven woods.

She must have slept. When she opened her eyes she was aware of a night-light on the wall of the cabin and the throb of the engines somewhere many metres below. She got up, banging her head on the bunk above. It was empty, just as it had been when

she came in, its laundered sheets folded in a neat
pile on top of the coverlet. Dan must be sleeping
elsewhere. Judi frowned. She groped her way to
the door and opened it. The corridor stretched impersonally on either side, a row of closed doors
giving no clue to the occupants of the cabins within.
She went back inside and lay down. Everyone must
be asleep. She would have to wait until morning to
find out where they were going. Had someone called
her family? When could she get to speak to them?
What about Dan? Would they like him? She hoped
so. Now she'd found the man she was going to
marry they would surely forgive her for everything.

There was a great deal of activity when she next
opened her eyes. The captain's wife was smiling.
'You're not coming all the way with us,' she told
her. 'The company has sent a helicopter from the
mainland, and I expect there'll be a flight from there
to take you back home. You must be so excited at
the thought of seeing all your dear ones again.'

'Yes... Yes, I am,' said Judi, opening her eyes
and trying to take in this new turn of events. 'Helicopter?' she asked. 'The oil company?'

'Your husband's company,' said the captain's
wife. 'He's been in communication with them all
night. What a sensation! It's going to be all over
the papers!'

Evidently the captain's wife thought Dan was her
husband—already! It seemed a good omen, despite
her confusion about what was actually going on
just now.

Judi showered again—it was a luxury to ease
away all the ingrained salt and grime of living

rough. She even washed her hair again, and regarded herself silently in the mirror. It hung to her shoulders in a soft curtain, making her look like a waif. Dan said he liked it long. At the time she had thought, He would, wouldn't he? and she remembered all the other hard things they had said to each other at the beginning. No one would have thought love could have blossomed in such unpromising soil. But there it was.

She put on the scratchy blouse and skirt and knickers again, and looked forward to seeing him. Eventually the captain's wife took her along the network of corridors and they finished up on the bridge. It was full of men, strangers in short-sleeved white shirts standing around a lot of flashing screens with disembodied robot voices keeping up a constant commentary. The men turned as Judi came in, and after a pause one of them stepped forward. He wore a cap covered in gold braid and held out his hands, saying something about how delighted she must be after such a long time to find herself back in the real world.

Then one of the strangers stepped forward and peered into her face. 'Did you sleep well?'

She had to look twice before she realised it was Dan. His bushy black beard had been cut short, and now it was little more than a dark stubble all over, revealing the strong jaw she remembered from their first encounter. The lovely long hair on his head had been neatly clipped to a more conventional length too, but it was something else that made him look like a stranger.

'You look different in clothes,' she blurted, then blushed when everybody laughed. Dan's lips tight-

TAKE FOUR
BEST SELLER ROMANCES
FREE!

♥

Best Sellers are for the true romantic! These stories are our favourite Romance titles re-published by popular demand.

♥

And to introduce to you this superb series, we'll send you four Best Sellers absolutely FREE when you complete and return this card.

♥

We're so confident that you will enjoy Best Sellers that we'll also reserve a subscription for you to the Mills & Boon Reader Service, which means you could enjoy...

♥

Four new novels sent direct to you every two months (before they're available in the shops).

Free postage and packing we pay all the extras.

Free regular Newsletter packed with special offers, competitions, author news and much, much more.

CLAIM YOUR FREE GIFTS OVERLEAF

MILLS & BOON
FREEPOST
P.O. BOX 236
CROYDON
CR9 9EL

Offer expires 31st. December 1992. The right is reserved to
change the terms of this offer or refuse an application. Readers
overseas and in Eire please send for details. Southern Africa write
to: Book Services International Ltd., P.O. Box 41654, Craighall,
Transvaal 2024. You may be mailed with offers from other reputable
companies as a result of this application. If you would

FREE BOOKS CERTIFICATE

YES! Please send me my four **FREE** Best Sellers together with my **FREE** gifts. Please also reserve me a special Reader Service subscription. If I decide to subscribe, I shall receive four superb Best Sellers every other month for just £6.40 postage and packing free. If I decide not to subscribe I shall write to you within 10 days. Any **FREE** books and gifts will remain mine to keep. I understand that I am under no obligation whatsoever - I may cancel or suspend my subscription at any time simply by writing to you. *I am over 18 years of age.*   4A2B

MS/MRS/MISS/MR

ADDRESS

POSTCODE _____ SIGNATURE

POST TODAY
and we'll send you this
cuddly Teddy Bear.

**PLUS a free
mystery gift!**
we all love mysteries, so as
well as the **FREE** books and
cuddly Teddy, there's an
intriguing mystery gift
specially for you.

ened. He was in a white short-sleeved shirt and
sharply pressed white trousers like the other men.
He could have been one of them, she thought before
she remembered that was what he was—in so-called
real life. She tried to smile, but her lips were trembling for some reason, so instead she looked down
at her bare feet and wondered what was the matter
with her.

'It'll take time to readjust,' said the captain
kindly. 'But you'll soon be back home!'

A messenger appeared at the door and said
something, and Judi felt herself shepherded off the
bridge and out on deck.

'This is it,' said Dan. 'No hanging about. You'll
be back home this time tomorrow.' There was a
helicopter, quite small compared to the ship itself.
She was handed up.

'What happened to the shoes?' he asked briskly
as soon as they were belted in. 'Couldn't they find
you any?' He turned to smile down at her as the
helicopter swooped sickeningly into the air. He gave
what she read as a stranger's smile, with his neat
beard and trimmed hair, a smile that meant
nothing. 'Never mind,' he said before she could
reply, 'soon be back to civilisation. You'll have all
the shoes you want then.'

'Dan,' she said, trying to slip her hand in his,
but drawing back as he turned to look down at the
carpet of blue scudding endlessly like a conveyor
belt beneath them. 'Dan, it's all so confusing.' Her
voice was a whisper of its usual self.

He was looking out of the window. 'You heard
what the captain said—it's going to take time to
readjust. Don't worry, once you're back with your

family this will seem like a dream.' He turned, still smiling. How could he, though, how could he talk of dreams, she asked herself, when they were leaving them behind for good?

'Dan,' she began again, 'I don't think I want it to be a dream . . . do you?'

He looked down at her, deep into her eyes, in a way that made her insides melt, but his eyes were glittering with a new excitement, a look she had never seen before. She read it as the prospect of challenge. 'I want one thing,' he confirmed. 'Right now the *only* thing I want is to be back where I belong.' He paused and a frown furrowed his brow. 'I'll tell you something, Judi—it's as if somebody has stolen six months from my life. And I want it back!' He gripped her hand hard in his own. 'There's going to be one hell of a lot of living to do to catch up. I can't wait!'

Judi gazed out at the measureless blue of sea and sky. There wasn't an island in sight.

She felt as if she had been turned to stone. There was a deadness inside her. Why couldn't she share in Dan's excitement? It was because he seemed to exclude her. Not once had he mentioned plans for the future that would involve her. He wanted to get back to his old life—he had said so. He couldn't wait. It was all that mattered. He spoke as if the last six months had been an interlude to the main show, something he had simply been forced to endure.

But for herself nothing had changed. The last six months had been only what her previous life had been leading up to, it was reality, and now she was being handed back into a world of make-believe.

Couldn't Dan see that? Why was he so taken with the life he had vowed could never mean anything to him?

The view remained unchanged until the pencil line of the mainland appeared in the east. Dan gave a shout. 'There she is—home, sweet home!' He peered jubilantly through the window. 'I'm flying straight to New York,' he told Judi. 'And I've arranged for you to pick up a flight to London. Your father was on the line last night, but we didn't want to wake you. There'll be quite a reception committee waiting for you!' He bent over her. 'Give me a kiss, angel. And thanks for keeping me sane. Good luck!'

Before Dan climbed down from the helicopter on to the landing pad there was a brief pause while they waited for the props to slow, then came a moment of silence and the doors were unlocked to let him swing down first on to the tarmac. Judi hesitated in the doorway, preparing to climb after him, but before she could take the first step a mob of reporters appeared, surrounding him with a yelling barrage of questions. She saw him put up a hand to screen his face from the cameras and turn to shout something up to her which she didn't catch, then the pilot pulled her back into the cockpit.

'Let him get away first,' he advised. 'He'll take the heat off.'

A hasty glance below showed her that Dan was already carving his way to a waiting car. He seemed to possess all the arrogance of a man used to handling the Press; it sent a small shock through her to witness the authority with which he faced them. It was as if he'd been doing this sort of thing all his life. Here was a hint that the Dan she knew was a stranger. She watched in a sort of daze as his dark head receded with the mob in his wake.

Her glance followed him all the way until he reached the car that was coming out from in front of the airport building to pick him up. When it slowed she saw him push through the last of the reporters and duck his head to get into the back seat. The door closed and the car began to force its way through the crowd. It was the car they had both been supposed to leave in. But he hadn't looked back.

'OK, out you go!' said the pilot, breaking into her thoughts and giving her a little push.

Relatively unnoticed, she was accompanied only by the pilot as she made her way across the tarmac into a side-entrance of a single-storey building.

She gazed round the arrivals hall in confusion. It was the first time she'd set foot inside a building for six months, and it was strangely claustrophobic. The ceiling seemed to be coming down on top of her head. And Dan was nowhere in sight.

Just before they landed he had repeated the fact that there was a connection for Heathrow from the public airport, adding, 'If there are any problems when we land, you go on ahead, otherwise you may miss your flight.' Not understanding what he meant, she'd protested, but he'd been firm. 'These South American schedules are sometimes erratic, and you don't want to be hanging around a city like this by yourself for longer than necessary.'

'But what about you, Dan?' she'd ventured to ask. 'How shall I find you in a strange airport?'

'I've already told you, I'm flying straight on to New York. By private jet,' he'd added. He had glanced out of the window as the outskirts of the city came into view below.

'You mean,' she'd paused, 'you mean this is goodbye?' Her lips felt suddenly stiff. What on earth was he saying? All the premonitions at his casual leavetaking of their island found a focus. Her startled glance had met his, but he gave her a brief, decisive smile that didn't reach his eyes.

'Not goodbye—I'll see you before your flight leaves.' He must have thought she was going to argue at having to go on alone, because he'd said quickly, 'I shall be leaving from here, but I'll come over to the international airport to see you off. OK?'

'But why the rush? Why can't we spend a few days in a hotel or something, getting used to being back and——' Being together, she'd meant. In a proper bed. With chance to talk about the future, for there were a lot of things to be discussed ... things that she hadn't had time to broach because of the speed with which they had been rescued.

But Dan had said, 'I can't hang around, don't you understand? I don't have the time. I have to get back. Responsibilities,' he'd added cryptically. 'It's going to be tricky getting back into the driving seat. God alone knows what's been happening in my absence. It'll be like coming back from the dead.'

'But——'

'I'll explain later.' His fingers had skimmed her bare arm. As Judi had noticed earlier, his body was taut with excitement, but this time there was nothing sexual in it. Desire seemed to be the last thing on his mind. It was simply because he was dying to get back, to don the trappings of his old life as soon as possible. All those lies about none of it being real any more were just that—lies. And she had fallen for them, every one! Nothing would deflect him now. She could tell just by looking at him. He was nearly emitting sparks with his impatience to be back. It made her feel shut out and alone, trapped in the prison of the past with secret thoughts he no longer wanted to share.

She'd felt like shouting at him, demanding to know what was so wonderful about the outside world, about deserting paradise. But she couldn't speak; her heart was too full. It was raw with a thousand splinters of pain.

And already they had been circling the landing strip. Soon they would be down.

Moments later she had watched him descend the steps.

Then the reporters had fallen on him, and he'd driven off without a backward glance. And Judi found herself in the almost empty arrivals lounge. There was no sign of him. He had gone, and she was alone.

Dan, she said over and over again. She felt numb, bereft of thought. Betrayed.

CHAPTER SEVEN

SOMEHOW or other Judi found herself on the far side of the city approaching the international airport with all its lines of lights and the great jumbo jets roaring in to land like predatory prehistoric monsters. Something already told her there would be no sign of Dan when she got there, so she was unsurprised when she failed to see his dark head among the crowd.

She was in a daze. Everything seemed to have been planned without any consultation. But then that was Dan all over. She told herself she shouldn't be surprised, everything was under control. But it was only a phrase to comfort herself when, secretly, she knew everything was lost.

To add to her confusion the mêlée of unfamiliar sights and sounds was alarming after the silence and tranquillity of the island. The city seemed to be a seething cauldron of flashing lights and music and bubbling, vociferous humanity. She couldn't make sense of it. Her head was spinning already. Why was everything moving so fast? What was it for? Why couldn't everyone slow down?

A hostess met her at the entrance to the departure lounge and she was led into the first-class section. Nobody mentioned air tickets. She let them take care of her because that was what they seemed to expect. She supposed her father had fixed things. She frowned at the thought of the reception com-

mittee awaiting her at home. She was longing to
see everyone; if it hadn't been for Dan she would
have missed them all far more. But she wondered
if things were going to be the same when she got
back. If Patrick still expected her to marry him. If
her father still had the same attitude to her career
as before.

Somehow the thought of Dan made all that seem
insignificant. This present mix-up must sort itself
out and everything would be back the way she imagined it, with Dan coming over to England to meet
her family. He would talk to her father. Everything
would be all right. He would help—she knew that.
She could rely on him.

The hostess was coming towards her now with a
bright professional smile on her face, offering
coffee, sandwiches, newspapers, then a few minutes
later ordering her politely towards the departure
doors.

'But I can't leave yet——' Judi protested. 'I'm
waiting for Dan.' Would they know who Dan was?
It appeared not. Although the hostess appeared to
speak excellent English she merely smiled and
nodded with no sign of comprehension in her eyes,
and Judi found herself being ushered firmly to the
doors.

Outside she could see the lights of the transcon-
tinental aircraft on the runway ready for take-off,
and when the time came she reluctantly allowed
herself to be led towards it, all the while shooting
glances over her shoulder in the hope that at the
last minute Dan's dark head would appear through
the crowd. But it didn't.

Soon she was on board, the pre-flight routine was under way, and then with a crushing roar they were airborne.

Dan, she cried inwardly, Dan, where are you? Why didn't you come to find me? Where are you? But there was no answer, and as she saw the lights of the city fall away it was as if half of herself had been ripped away too.

She slept on the flight to Europe. It was the only way she knew to shut out the increasing miles that separated them.

'Daddy! Mummy!... And Sarah! Oh, my precious loves...' The arms of her family came round her and feelings long forgotten brought tears to her eyes. 'I can't begin to tell you what it was like. It was amazing—terrifying, wonderful, extraordinary!' She was laughing and crying at the same time. Sarah gave her a special hug.

'Glad my big sister's home to boss me about—I really missed you!' She shook Judi by the shoulders. 'Love the tan! You look fantastic!' They hugged each other all the way to the waiting car.

Her father punched his driver on the arm when they got there, an unprecedented familiarity that showed how delighted he was to have his daughter back home where she belonged. 'Get us out of here, Jimmy,' he ordered. 'The Press are baying at the gates.' They had rushed her off the plane to a separate exit, but even as he spoke a few newspapermen separated themselves from the crowd and ran towards the car. They were left gazing furiously after their disappearing tail-lights in a repetition of the scene when Dan had made a similar getaway.

'Well, sweetheart, you've had quite an adventure. More than you bargained for, eh?' Charles de Burgh leaned across the back of the seat in front and gave Judi a searching glance. She nodded.

'It was awful not knowing anything, darling.' Her mother gripped her hands in hers. 'They published the names of the ones who were missing—then tried to tell us not to give up hope. You seemed to have vanished off the face of the earth. They told me that was a good sign—no news is good news.' Her mother's eyes glistened.

'I'm sorry—I really am. I shouldn't have gone off like that, without telling you where I was going. Everything simply got too much for me here...'

'We understand.' Winnie de Burgh gave her husband a meaningful look and held Judi's hand in hers.

'I'm glad to be home,' whispered Judi. 'I thought about you all every day. I thought I'd never see any of you again.' Her mind went back to the family row that had led to her hurried departure. It seemed like something that had happened to someone else, someone who no longer existed. And she knew she had been forgiven long ago. It was plain to see in their welcome.

'You got on the wrong track, that's all, darling.' Her mother linked her arm in hers. 'You were always headstrong. But now you're back safe and sound, and in years to come maybe we'll see what happened as a sort of blessing in disguise.' She looked at Judi's younger sister. Judi saw the look and realised that Sarah too had changed in the last six months. But time for that later.

'Something good has come out of it,' she agreed. 'If I hadn't taken that ridiculous job on the cruise ship and if it hadn't blown up, I would never have met Dan.'

Home was an Elizabethan manor house in the Thames valley. A few friends formed a reception committee on the drive, and Judi was subjected to more hugs and squeals of delight when she climbed out of the car. One of the air hostesses had lent her a pair of shoes, but she was still wearing the blouse and skirt the captain's wife had given her, and she felt awkward, like someone playing a part in a play.

When she had greeted everyone she turned at the top of the steps. 'Look, I'm wild at seeing you all again. I still can't quite believe it, but less than thirty-six hours ago I was living on a coral atoll!' Her throat contracted inexplicably and she tried to turn it into a laugh. 'Now, well——' she paused and managed to clear her throat '—well, I'm home. What more can I say?' She shot a helpless glance towards her mother.

'I'm giving everyone supper in the kitchen and then I think I'll have to ask you all to go home. Judi's had a gruelling experience, and I'm going to pack her off to her room for a good night's sleep as soon as I can.' Mrs de Burgh was firm underneath the dithery charm.

Judi squeezed her hand. 'I feel as if this is all some kind of a dream. It's overwhelming—it's quite unreal.' As everyone moved towards the kitchen she stood undecidedly in the hall. Where was Dan? She felt as if she was someone else, a stranger in the midst of strangers. Did she really know all these people? She turned towards the stairs. 'I'm sorry,' she said, when someone tried to make her stay, 'I just want to be alone.' She turned and began to climb towards her room, managing to look back at the first turn to say, 'I'll—I'll see you all tomorrow. Thanks for being here.'

Later, when everyone had gone, she went down again. She couldn't sleep. Her mind was buzzing with all the sights and sounds of civilisation, and she longed for the peace and quiet of the island. But most of all she longed for Dan. His absence was like a physical wound. Half of her was missing, and she couldn't rest until she felt whole again. Nothing was real without Dan.

Charles de Burgh was in the sitting-room when she opened the door.

'Come in, my darling. Let me have a look at you.' She stood before him as he took her by the shoulders. 'You're looking remarkably well after such an ordeal,' he observed after giving her a thorough assessment. 'Chip off the old block, eh?'

She nodded and gave him one of her old, quick smiles. She and her father had once understood each other. Maybe it was something to do with growing up and becoming independent that had led to friction. But he seemed to have forgotten all that, for he said, 'Come and talk?'

She nodded. 'Is there a lot to talk about?'

He pulled out a chair. 'Sit down—I don't want you to fall down when I tell you what I'm going to say.'

Judi lifted her head.

'Put this on record,' he began with a smile. 'I was wrong.'

'Dad?' She gave a start. It was unheard-of for her father to admit being wrong about anything. He and Dan were alike in that respect. 'You mean you were wrong about Patrick and wanting me to marry him?' she asked.

He shook his head. 'That's not the episode uppermost in my mind—though I accept that I was wrong to insist on that too. I simply thought you were getting cold feet and needed a little push. I hadn't realised that it went deeper than that. Anyway,' he continued, 'that's your mother's department. You and Patrick—and Sarah—will have to sort it out among yourselves.' He paused, and before she could ask what Sarah had to do with it he went on, 'No, I mean the other matter—your ambition to be part of de Burgh. I was wrong not to give you a chance, almost unforgivably wrong. You're a bright young woman, but I guess I was stuck in a time-warp, thinking a daughter of mine in the latter half of the twentieth century would be happy being a stay-at-home housewife when there are worlds to conquer. There, I've said it. You were right to resist, right not to give in. I'm sorry. Forgive me?'

'Oh, *Dad*...!' Judi didn't know whether to laugh or cry. Life on the island had almost obliterated one of the major reasons that had sent her running away all those months ago.

The ensuing months of strife, days when she and her father had treated each other with icy silence, weeks when she had skipped out of college because, without the prospect of a career at the end of it, there was simply no point in going on attending lectures, weeks of family arguments, the endless discussions, and the brick wall of her father's will which she had smashed herself against endlessly without hope... and now he was saying he was wrong!

He was smiling at her. Slowly, in case she'd *still* got it wrong, she said, 'You mean you'll let me join the company? I mean, you'll actually let me work for you...? You think I can do it?' When she saw his expression she gave a little cry and flung herself across the room into his arms. 'You mean it? You'll really give me a chance to prove myself?'

His arms came round her and he gave her a brief hug, then took her by the shoulders. 'It is still what you want, isn't it? It wasn't just a teenage whim?' His grey eyes searched her face, but she allayed his doubts at once.

'It's what I prayed and hoped for—you know it is. Ever since I was a little girl I've loved nothing better than playing around with figures. Remember how I used to haunt your office, getting under everyone's feet?'

'I remember you at twelve, popping up asking questions at every turn. I loved it. But I never thought it would last. I thought you'd turn out like your mother, bless her.'

'I'm not. I'm like you,' Judi said proudly. She was scarcely able to speak for happiness. For a moment she almost forgot the pain of Dan's absence. 'You always knew it was my dearest ambition to work for de Burgh,' she told him. 'I'll start at the bottom—anything! I just know I can do it. I know I can be good.'

'I know it too. I have complete faith in you—I always had. It's just that I imagined a different sort of future for my beautiful daughter. I wanted a life of pleasure for you—without the stress and strain of holding down a demanding position with the company. Now I know nothing less will satisfy you.'

'You really believe I can be good?'

'I know it. But I've already lined up your first assignment. You're going to have a proper chance to show me what you can do.'

'What is it?' Judi's eyes were beginning to uncloud and for a few brief moments she almost forgot the source of the pain that was shredding her heart to ribbons, but her father waved her away.

'Later. You've just flown halfway across the world. Get some rest now. We'll talk in a couple of days when I've worked out the details, and then you can give me your whole attention.'

She left him then, and in the privacy of her room she gazed at all the half-familiar things—books and ornaments and old toys she had forgotten about. There was an air of unreality about it all, as if the teddy bear on the shelf had belonged to some other child, the silver tennis cups not hers, the riding rosettes another girl's. She picked up a school photograph and gazed uncomprehendingly at the gap-toothed twelve-year-old, then at the photograph in the silver frame of the young man she had been supposed to marry. She hoped he wasn't hurt, but he had seemed to understand how she felt about the marriage that was being arranged between them.

Yawning, she lay down on her bed, her pain at Dan's inexplicable rejection tempered with a mixture of surprise at being back in the middle of the old life she had half forgotten and joy that, contrary to what she had half expected, the fight with her father was over. As soon as Dan was beside her again life would be complete.

She gave a little laugh of pure happiness when she remembered what it was she had to tell him.

Surely the confusion of their leavetaking would be resolved within the next few hours? Then she would feel truly blessed, with his loving arms around her once again. Dan! Her beloved hero. The man who had saved her life and now gave it meaning.

She couldn't wait to see him again. It had been wrong of her to have such black thoughts about him simply because circumstances beyond their control had ripped them both apart before they were prepared. They would meet as soon as they had sorted out the ragged ends of their old lives. She was impatient, but she could wait.

She was just drifting off when there was a soft knock on the door.

'It's me.' Sarah poked her head round and looked in. 'You weren't asleep already, were you?' She came in and sat down on the bed when she saw Judi was still awake.

Judi gave a yawn, followed by a rueful smile. 'Almost—I'm almost too tired to think. But I'm glad you've come up.' She paused. 'Has Patrick forgiven me for running away?'

'He's still waiting.' Sarah averted her glance. 'He haunts this place. He always said he knew you'd survive.'

'Oh, no...' Judi slumped back. 'I haven't gone through the last six months to finish up marrying a man like Patrick!'

'He's really sweet. You were always so rotten to him!' Sarah bit her lip. 'I'm sorry—I never have understood why you don't like him.'

'I *like* him. I just don't fancy him. I don't——' Judi corrected, 'I don't love him to distraction.'

'You are a romantic! So it still has to be all or nothing?'

'Of course! I told you it could be different from whatever Patrick and I had.' And now I've proved it, Judi wanted to add, but a sudden foreboding made her hold the words back.

'What was this Dan like you were stranded with?' Sarah watched her expression.

Judi gave a half-smile, closing her eyes, a fleeting image of the last time she had seen Dan momentarily clouding the blissful memory of the sweet secret things about him she could never tell anyone else.

'I guess you must really get to know someone well when you spend six whole months alone with them.' Sarah went on, 'I even got to know Patrick rather well—despite a stream of chaperons!'

But Judi was only half listening. Her mind was on Dan. She missed him, she missed him like mad. It was an ache in the depths of her being, longing for him as much as this and being unable to contact him. Everything had happened too quickly. Obviously his plans had gone wrong, despite his usual super-efficiency. He must have been as confused as she was about the practicalities of bringing their old lives into the same orbit. It was as if the

world had split in two, and at present there was no
bridge between the separate halves. But Dan would
find a way.

She wanted to explain to Sarah, because she
sensed she would understand, but she was too tired
to talk, and, almost before her sister left the room,
her eyes were beginning to close.

Next morning Sarah was back, bouncing into Judi's
room with a breakfast tray—together with a pile of
newspapers. 'They're all full of the heroine's return,
and we've had a constant barrage of photographers
and reporters at the gates since the early hours.
You'll have to agree to talk to one of them just to
keep them quiet. I think they want to offer you a
lot of money for your story.'

Judi groaned and rolled over. Despite the excitement of being home she had gone out like a
light last night, but now her young sister was
searching rapidly through the papers. 'Look at
this!' she said. 'Brilliant picture! You looking out
of the back window of the car,' she announced,
throwing them down one by one on the bed so Judi
could see them. 'You look like some fugitive movie
star! And another one here with your head down.
Dad nearly bashed that chap with his own camera!'
Sarah threw the paper down on top of the pile, then
announced, 'And from the other side of the
Atlantic—the *New York Times*!' she announced.
'Just get him! You didn't tell me your beach-mate
was such a hunk!' She threw another paper on to
the bed with a flourish.

Judi snatched it up. There he was, Dan, her
darling, darling Dan, grinning out at the camera,

looking more relaxed than he had when they parted
and impossibly glamorous, with his tan obvious
even in black and white! He had already had his
hair cut, and the roughly trimmed beard he had
worked on with a pair of scissors every now and
then was thinned down to a hint of attractive de-
signer stubble. If anything he looked more
handsome, more rakish, more desirable than ever.
I love you, she thought with a jolt of longing as
she scanned the caption. Then she gasped out loud.

'What's the matter?' Sarah leaned forward to
take the paper, but Judi snatched it back.

'Constantine Daniels,' she read silently, 'jet-
setting tycoon, back from the dead ... to the arms
of fiancée Jo Lee.' Her eyes blurred and she heard
the paper crackle beneath her fingers. 'Go away,
Sarah,' she managed to mutter, 'I'm still half
asleep.' She dropped face down in the pillow, bur-
rowing under it as if she could blot out what she
had just read.

When she heard the door close she slowly lifted
her head and read the item properly. It wasn't a
misreading at all. That was what it really said: his
fiancée. But then why should he have mentioned a
fiancée when he hadn't even told her his real name?
And *tycoon*? What did that mean? He was a sailor
on a cruise ship, wasn't he? At least, that was the
conclusion Judi had jumped to in those early days,
and he hadn't corrected her. Constantine. Constant.
Constant in love? She felt like throwing up.

She was still lying face down when her mother
came in to see if she wanted anything else. Because
it was her first day back they were treating her like
an invalid.

From beneath the duvet she said, 'Mum, I've been thinking about that Press interview Sarah mentioned. Get somebody to fix one for me, would you? It sounds fun.' No wonder he hadn't shown up at the airport to kiss her a fond goodbye—not with all the cameras waiting to record the event for the fiancée waiting patiently back home! And now she knew what the 'responsibilities' were that he had vaguely mentioned.

Her mother gave her a glance of surprise. 'Are you sure you want to be bothered with that sort of thing just yet?'

Judi nodded. It would take her mind off the slow fracturing of her heart. Anything would be better than thought. If she allowed herself to think of the present she'd die. And anyway, it was Dan himself who had encouraged her to fight back. She'd show him! When she had first opened her eyes after nearly drowning and seen his enigmatic face hovering above hers she had felt helpless, and somehow she had known even then that he could annihilate her. Here was the proof. Yet if it was to happen, she would go down fighting. She was a de Burgh. And nobody, not Dan, nor Constantine, not anybody, would ever ultimately destroy her. For she had something more precious to live for than he would ever know.

'So tell me again how you managed to do the cooking,' asked the journalist from the woman's page of the national daily that had won the race to interview her. 'Did you share it between the two of you, or was that your job while Tine did all the more macho chores?'

Tine. They called him Tine. It made him sound like a stranger—like the stranger he really was. Judi felt she was developing a split personality—talking about one man, while everybody else was talking about another. She discovered he was a shipping tycoon. That and many other interests to do with communications. Ironic, really—he'd been travelling incognito on one of his own newly acquired ships. There had been bomb threats. It was like him to be there at the scene. And no wonder he had been furious at failing to make contact with the outside world. *Communications*. Judi had to laugh. That was the one area in which he was a hopeless failure.

Her Dan, the one who had said all those crazy, romantic things about moon goddesses, had been left on the island. All that remained was this ruthless millionaire called Tine. From among the shards of a broken heart she was vainly trying to piece back her image of Dan. It was confusing. It couldn't be done. He had died on the island the minute strangers had set foot on it.

She was glad, though, that Tine would eventually read the article describing her own experiences on Love Island. It would balance the accounts she had read of his time there.

Love Island! There was a lot being written about that—a stream of articles. The Press loved him. Well, he was photogenic, wasn't he? And rich. And about to marry his childhood sweetheart. How romantic! She was his press secretary, a girl from somewhere in Connecticut whose name Judi deliberately forgot.

It was interesting, she told herself, to read *his*
version of events. About his longing to get off Hell
Island. About how his determination to get home
to his loved one had sustained him. About the dif-
ficulties he had had to face, never-ending and made
worse by having a helpless female to look after.
Well, he hadn't put it quite like that, but that was
the gist.

Now she gave *her* version. The difficulty of living
with a man who didn't understand women, who
made her feel like crawling under a stone and giving
up, but against whom she had learned to fight in
order to survive. The physical hardships had been
nothing compared to the social ones, having to learn
to get on with a brutish, insensitive stranger. How
the thought of getting away from him had kept her
going.

The worst thing, she said, to an interviewer from
a style magazine, was having to take survival so
seriously! Heavens, she said, how men go on about
the boring little details! We'd have survived anyway.
Nothing to it—plenty of fruit and fish, marvellous
climate. But Tine—she smiled, and the photographer had managed to catch that look Dan had
described as coquettish—Tine was the sort of man
to take everything seriously. Not boring exactly, but
rather dull. Quite a competent man and useful to
have around. Good for carrying heavy objects and
re-erecting collapsed tents.

But she couldn't describe how delighted she
was—yes, ecstatic, to be back in grimy old London.
She'd so missed the nightlife.

He was one of those men, she added as a way of
signing off, who simply glory in pretending to be

macho. They love discomfort for its own sake. The backwoods type. Some men are like that, aren't they?

The photographer caught that look again, and when he left he said, 'It's going to be a great picture, darlin'!'

'That was rather harsh,' said Sarah as she read the article over breakfast later on. 'I didn't get the impression you felt like that about him. It must have been hell.' The fact that he hadn't been in touch received no comment from anyone. Perhaps they all put it down to the general confusion caused by their sudden reappearance as if from the dead.

'I thought I did feel something,' said Judi shortly, 'but the emotions play funny tricks when you're cooped up with the same person for months on end. Afterwards it doesn't mean a damned thing. Just like a holiday romance.' She got up. 'I'm going for a ride.' Dad was coming back early that evening. Instead of their talk about her future he had had to leave for the office before she was awake. But he had timetabled her in, said his message when she got up, for late that afternoon. She would ride, clear her mind, concentrate on the future. There was every reason now to think ahead.

'Judi de Burgh? I have a call for you.'

Before she could slam the receiver down painfully familiar tones, ones she had longed to hear, vibrated down the line. 'Judi? It's me. I'm going to be in London towards the end of the week. Where will you be?'

'Me? Who is that, exactly?'

'Dan, of course. Didn't you recognise my voice?'

'Dan? Oh—Dan,' she feigned, as if she hadn't been thinking of him constantly ever since they'd parted.

'Well, what about it?' He sounded impatient.

She could hear the sound of conversation in the background. 'What about what?' she stalled.

'Lunch,' he replied, a sharper tone coming into his voice.

Her thoughts raced. She couldn't face him—it was no good. It would be a slanging match. Now she had discovered the truth about him they could have nothing to say to each other that wasn't slanderous. 'I'm going away for a few days——' she said lamely. It was obvious to anyone that she was inventing excuses on the spur of the moment.

He ignored her and said, 'I think we should meet soon.'

Recovering a little, she said as cuttingly as she could, 'You do?'

Her voice sounded weird, as if she had a cold and had to clear her throat, and by that time he was saying, 'I don't know what it's been like with you, but it's been hell here. Anyway, I've got everything under control for the moment, so I suggest Brown's, lunch, three days hence.' He sounded sharp and very busy.

'That's rather short notice,' she demurred. There was a war going on inside her—a desperate longing to see him again, if only for a moment, and the horror at meeting the man she loved now that she knew he was to marry someone else. Somehow or other she managed to say, 'I'll have to have a look at my book.' There was no book. She hadn't given a thought to the social scene yet, nor did she expect to.

'Well, if you can't make it I'll just have to drive out to see you.'

'Pressuring me, are you?'

'Is that how you see it?' He sounded annoyed.

There was a long silence. Judi couldn't bring herself to lie to him, but nor could she give him the satisfaction of knowing how much she longed to hold him in her arms again, fiancée or not.

Oh, Dan, she thought feverishly, where are you? Aloud she said, 'It's been so confusing. There seems to be so much to catch up on. I've hardly been anywhere since I got back.'

'Except for night-clubbing, of course.' He paused as if inviting her to deny any such thing, but she didn't, and he went on offhandedly, 'I suppose I shall have to send a car or something.'

Obviously he'd already read that interview she'd done. Did it mean he had been scouring the English newspapers as she'd been scouring the American ones? But then she remembered the tame press officer, and it made sense to think that any reference that put her fiancé's Love Island companion in a bad light would land pretty damned quick on his desk. Her fingers clenched round the receiver. 'You're wasting your time if you imagine you can organise me the way you did before,' she said, matching his offhand tone as closely as she could. 'We're not on Love Island any longer. Now I arrange my own life, thank you very much.'

'Yes, of course.' His voice was flat. 'But I hope you'll make a real effort to see me.'

Not on your life, she thought, as she rang off. It was no good. Even a second's thought told her how impossible it would be to be face to face with him again. She simply wasn't tough enough, brash enough, hard-boiled enough. God, she thought, stuffing a fist into her mouth to force back a sob, how can I go on like this? She was aware that he was turning her into a quivering jelly of emotion, just when she should be at her most calm and resolute.

By the time she saw Jimmy driving her father up the drive towards the house that evening Judi had schooled herself into showing none of the turmoil raging just beneath the surface. She went to the door to greet him.

'Agog to hear what I have lined up for you?' he demanded with a smile as he climbed up the steps and gave her a peck on the cheek. 'That's my girl,' he said, going swiftly on into the house.

She followed him into the sitting-room and poured him a drink. 'Well?' she asked as she went towards him with a plastic smile on her face. Work was the antidote to Constantine Daniel. Work and more work. She would erase him from her mind and from her life. She would leave no room for him. She lifted her face expectantly.

'Slow down!' her father joked. 'You may not feel like jetting off so soon after all you've been through, but that's what it might entail, I'm afraid.'

'Don't worry about that,' she told him quickly. 'I can't wait to get involved. I've lost six months of my life,' she added, recalling Dan's words as they left the oil tanker.

'You won't object to flying out to New York next week, then?'

She shook her head, quelling the kick in the stomach his words gave her. New York was Tine's city. But she would get used to that.

He explained, 'We're being consulted by a Stateside group due to move into Europe later this year. There are one or two details best dealt with face to face about their overall funding—I've got the files here.' He patted his briefcase, then leaned down to open it. 'It'll appeal to you,' he said as he straightened up. 'The principal is not unknown.'

His words meant nothing to her until he pushed the file across and she held it in her hands. Even then it didn't sink in, until she opened it and came to the name at the bottom of the top document. Then she felt her cheeks blanch.

She had to read it twice, the letters dancing before her eyes. When she raised them to her father with the idea that it must be some kind of crazy joke his head was bent as he riffled through some more papers, and by the time he looked up she was in control again. Of course he couldn't know how she felt about Dan, about Tine. No one did. No one could.

'But why is——?' She couldn't trust herself to say his name aloud, so she started again. 'How is it you've been approached by——' she forced herself on '—by his company? I didn't know you had any connection with them.'

Her father beamed. 'It was through you, of course. When he rang me the night of the rescue we'd already heard of each other, naturally. He broached the possibility of using us when he got back to New York. A call from one of my executives the other day clinched things.'

'Through *me* . . .' Judi couldn't make sense of it. Somehow she felt she was the one who was being used. 'I see,' she managed. Why, oh, why? she asked herself inwardly. Fate, fortune, that was why. And Tine. Not letting an opportunity pass him by. Bowing to fortune. It seemed she couldn't evade its tricks and betrayals.

'Now you see why I want you to handle it for me?' her father went on, oblivious to her raging emotions. 'Who better? You know the man. He's halfway to saying yes already. And it's an excellent project on which to cut your teeth.'

She felt herself give a faint nod. Her palms had gone clammy and the pages jittered between her fingers as she made a pretence of scanning the underlying sheets. She allowed her father to talk, outlining what he wanted her to say, how to approach the meeting with Dan—with Tine; she must get used to calling him that. He talked about Tine's fellow directors, what to do to counter any objections that might arise, giving her a thorough briefing, unaware of how it was only sheer willpower that kept her seated before him instead of running from the room.

'That's that,' he said in conclusion. 'Are you happy?'

He meant, did she understand what he had told her, could she handle it. Happy? She gave a hollow-sounding laugh. 'Great—can't wait! When do I leave?' She got up and forced a remnant of a smile on to her face before fleeing.

*   *   *

Later, alone in her room, she realised why Tine had called and tried to fix lunch with her. Already knowing his company would be consulting her father's organisation, he had got around to ringing her merely in order to circumvent any problems that might arise by not doing so—business problems, that was. And she had been so stupidly naïve that, even with the existence of a fiancée in the background, she had nurtured a sneaking hope that his call might mean something more.

What a fool I am! What an utter, abject fool! She tortured herself with unending recriminations until at last some residual courage asserted itself and she found the strength to think only of the practicalities as they now faced her.

Above all was the need to make a success of the assignment her father had entrusted to her. Then she would tackle the other more personal problems, taking them one by one.

Before any of that could happen, though, there was the ordeal of coming face to face with Tine over lunch. The thought was terrifying. What if she broke down? She could just see the look of contempt on his face. His eyes would be like blue ice, as they had been when they first encountered each other. He had told her then he was no good with hysterical women.

There were only three days to go. Was it long enough to learn to conceal the broken heart that seemed to jut like a broken bone beneath the skin?

CHAPTER EIGHT

SARAH and her mother were standing on the steps to wave goodbye when a few days later Judi was ready to go up to London. 'You look fantastic,' approved Sarah after inspecting the new clothes she had splurged on. 'Very chic! I'm quite in awe of you.'

'You should treat me with respect now I'm a business tycoon,' she quipped. 'And I'm older than you.' Her face betrayed nothing of the anguish she felt at the forthcoming ordeal.

Her mother pecked her on the cheek. 'Isn't that skirt rather short, darling?'

'It's all the style now,' said Judi, giving her a return peck, then adding a hug as well. She couldn't let them know how fast her heart was beating.

They watched the car out of sight, Sarah these days looking more contented than she had ever done. Judi knew the reason now: it was Patrick. That episode had sorted itself out very well. Her father was wary about trying to force his elder daughter into some dynastic marriage now, and even Patrick himself had forgiven her for running away from him and taking a job as a DJ on board that ill-fated cruise-liner. His bony, intelligent face had lost its look of hurt, and she knew he would be happier with somebody like Sarah. After they had had a talk he said, 'We were meant to be brother and sister, Judi, it's just that none of us thought of that at the time.'

'We grew up together, fell out of apple trees together, competed at gymkhanas together. How on earth could we also hope to live together?' Judi had said. 'It was Father's crazy idea that we should become husband and wife. His mania for tying up loose ends let him down!'

Now they were firm friends again, just as they had been when they were ten.

Thinking of Patrick—and Sarah—took Judi's mind off Tine. She refused to think about him until she reached the hotel.

It was as she pushed her way through the hotel doors that she caught her first glimpse of him.

Even though the foyer was busy with pre-lunch guests, she couldn't mistake that imposing physique. Tamed into a dark business suit, he still looked ferally sexy, like a prowling panther looking for a mate. He was eyeing the women who clipped by in their high heels, his glance never lingering for more than a second, until they suddenly swivelled, catching sight of Judi through the crowd. They levelled remorselessly on hers, and she felt a kick in the stomach that sent all thought flying out of her head. He seemed to hold her glance in a vice so that she couldn't tear her eyes away, and the hotel seemed to fall silent, though she knew it was only an illusion, because her own attention was all in what she saw.

He looks fantastic, she thought fatalistically. The dark suit was teamed with a dazzling shirt whose shade of broad blue stripes exactly matched his eyes. They were so blue, she registered, that they were like fragments of heaven, and she wondered how she could ever have forgotten that piercing look that could see straight into her soul with all its secrets and its longings and its present devastating pain.

Then it was as if the floor was opening up, for he was carving his way towards her. Tine. Dan. Judi put up a hand as if to ward him off. But he kept coming forward and the moment seemed to go on forever. Then he was standing in front of her, tall, dark, dangerous, beard gone now to reveal the hard jaw she remembered from their first ever meeting.

And all these hours apart she had been telling herself he was an illusion, someone she had invented to stop herself from going mad in paradise.

But he was here, and he was no illusion. Now the pleasure and the pain came together.

Putting out one very real hand, he gripped her by the wrist, his fingers circling it in a gesture of strange intimacy that made her recoil with the sharp shock of contact.

Noticing her withdrawal, he let his hand drop to his side. 'I scarcely recognised you.' His voice sent a thrill of longing through her. It was deeper, more masculine than she wanted to remember. He added, 'You've cut your hair.'

'Yes,' she found her voice, 'I seem to remember you don't particularly care for short hair.' The implication was obvious.

She saw his eyes harden. But why should she pretend? she asked herself. She had seen pictures of the fiancée, all floating tresses, dreamily romantic. She managed to preserve a plastic half-smile, but it seemed as if they were both taking stock. Beneath his cool expression she knew he was giving her a thorough-going assessment, and she knew he wouldn't like what he saw. He didn't like women who looked sleek and chic and knew what they were about. Tough, she thought defiantly. He had never really known her—just as she had never really known him, except in a physical sense. Yet she wished she weren't so aware of his physical presence now. He was overwhelming. In the civilised setting of the hotel, more even than in the barbaric wildness of the island, he seemed bigger, more powerful, more vibrant and, she had to admit it, more sexually lethal than ever. Heads turned even as they stood like this, staring into each other's hostile eyes.

'And lips are back in fashion too, I see.' His glance hovered over her mouth as if he wanted to taste it.

Judi gave him a cold glance and without smiling said, 'I hope you don't intend to dwell on my appearance? On the island I guessed you'd turn out to be that type of man, and despite the civilised and barbered look you seem to prove me right.' Before he could interrupt she went on, 'I'm here to do business. I should take a dim view of things if you didn't intend to take me seriously. Father expects me to get results.'

'Results?' He gave her a lazy smile and his voice dropped to a suggestive growl. 'Results are what I'm after too.' He made a deliberate pause and she saw the corners of his lips lift in an ironic smile, even though his eyes had become blank ice chips.

It was the look she recalled from those early days, first the provocative remark, then the withdrawal.

She felt her temper rise. She had been right about him all along. His patronising tone and the way his glance had lingered suggestively over her mouth just now showed he was the Neanderthal type who couldn't take women seriously. That was how he had been on the island—treating her like an imbecile just because she was female. He was going to have a shock, then, because although she wasn't very practical she had a good business head and a way with figures inherited from her father. She was on home ground this time, and she felt she could afford to smile. She did so, the word coquettish springing to mind and making her smile even more.

He wouldn't reduce her to a gibbering wreck again. She had had three days to school her emotions, and she would show him he couldn't whisper love into her ear one minute and cast her into oblivion the next. She would show him she was as tough as he was, as tough, as cold.

She lifted her head. 'Shall we go through?' she asked acidly. It was the firing of the first shot presaging war, and her intention was not lost on him. He seemed to flinch, probably in surprise, she judged, not expecting her to fight back but to fit in with whatever he had to suggest, just as she had been forced to do on the island. She was glad he'd got the picture, but at the same time she knew she had to tread carefully, for she was here as her father's emissary, and nothing was going to stand between her and success.

They stood looking at each other as awkwardly as strangers until Tine said briskly, 'Very well, as you wish. Let's join the others.' Judi gave a start which he was quick enough to notice. 'Unfortunately,' his tone was smooth, 'I'm with some other people.'

'I didn't realise anyone else was going to be involved,' she began in surprise, but when she saw him begin to give what she interpreted as a smug smile she went on, 'I thought this was a business meeting? One in which we're supposed to be discussing the possibility of your using us during your move into Europe? Do you mean I'm wasting my time?' She lifted her head in mock surprise.

His blue eyes froze over. 'We're testing the possibility of using you, yes.' He returned her stare.

'So it's not definite after all?' she persisted as coolly as she could. 'I understood it was?'

His lips tightened in a barely perceptible grimace. 'Is anything ever definite in real life?' he asked heavily.

'In business it is, I'm delighted to say.'

'The one constant, the business of making money?' He gave a wry smile. 'This throws a new light on things... Or does it?' He seemed about to go on, but instead took her by the elbow.

Pointedly detaching herself, Judi moved on ahead, then paused, unsure where they were to meet his other guests.

He was so close behind her he bumped into her, and she stepped back as if touched by an electric prod.

'Judi...' His voice was close to her ear, a murmur, an invitation, a caress. He stopped in mid-sentence, and she eyed him blankly. Why was he hinting that he still felt some of the old feeling when his eyes

were so guarded? His expression had no sign of
warmth in it. Was he hoping she would crack so
that he could use it as an excuse not to do business
with de Burgh after all? She had to prove that there
were going to be no complications, that it would
be business as usual, full steam ahead, no hassle.

'I'm sorry you haven't come to a final decision
to use us,' she said carefully. 'I assumed you were
going to go ahead. I hope it's nothing to do with
me, this hesitation.'

'You want me to use you?' His lips scarcely
moved.

Judi felt her breath draw in at the subtle implication behind his words. But no, she must be imagining it. She returned a level glance and said,
'Yes, very much.'

'Won't you find it difficult——' he paused,
choosing his words, '—in view of our previous
relationship?'

'I can't see what that has to do with it.'

'Because it was in the past?'

'Quite.'

He presented a dazzle of even teeth, a token smile
not extending to his eyes. 'What's past is past. Yes,
I remember a similar conversation we had once...'
He took her arm, this time firmly enough not to
allow her any escape, and said, 'We're keeping
everyone waiting. But rest assured, in view of what
you've just said I suspect I can easily sway my fellow
directors into using your services. We'll see how it
goes, shall we?'

Judi jerked her glance round to catch a confirmation of some further double meaning, but he was

already turning, one arm sliding round her waist to pull her after him through the crowd.

The fact that he hadn't even bothered to make time to see her alone, that he had merely tacked her into an already existent business meeting despite what they had gone through together, tore at her heart, but she followed him through into the dining-room with a face of masklike composure, even though her knees felt like buckling under her.

What she had planned to say to him after the meeting was finished was something that must be said in private. Now she wondered if there was any point. Some things were best left unsaid. And all those crazy things they had told each other on the island, for instance, were words which should never ever have been uttered.

Everything after that seemed to happen at one remove. First the introductions—Judi couldn't recall the names of a single one of the three other members of the group afterwards—then the courses of a perfectly served meal passing as inevitably as destiny until the brandy stage, and then somehow everything drawing to a close as two of the group began to rise to their feet.

Tine—it was definitely not Dan—moved with them towards the exit to see them out, and Judi and the other woman who had been present, the manager of a company doing business with one of Tine's companies, remained seated at the table, finishing their drinks.

'I'd like to get him on my own for a few minutes,' the woman said, leaning towards Judi. 'If I let him

slip out of the net now I'll have wasted weeks of
negotiations with his subordinates.'

'That's all right, I have to go anyway. Thank him
for the meal, would you?' On impulse, before she
could weaken and change her mind, Judi slipped
out of the dining-room by another door and hurried
into the hotel lobby.

What on earth was she doing, running away like
this? But then what on earth had made her agree
to meet Tine anyway? Without understanding her
own motives she had harboured the notion that it
was going to turn out to be some sort of reunion,
maybe only an affirmation, but something just to
show that, despite the demands of the so-called real
world, what had happened on the island had meant
something, that it hadn't been an illusion. But it
was obvious that his feelings had evaporated from
the moment the possibility of escape had appeared.

Everything till then had been a fantasy born of
the fear of being cast away forever and what simply
came down to sheer animal lust.

Judi gave a shudder. It wasn't true, it hadn't been
like that. Not a fantasy—not for herself.

She made her way in a sort of trance through the
revolving doors and out into the street, where she
hailed a cab. She sank back just as Tine—she was
finding it easier to call him that now—appeared on
the pavement outside the hotel. He looked quickly
up and down as the cab pulled away, then turned
and went back inside without seeing her.

'Goodbye,' she whispered. Tears gathered in the
corners of her eyes. 'Goodbye, Dan.'

*   *   *

'What the hell happened to you this lunchtime?'
The voice was irate and could belong to no one else.
'Apparently you left your thanks and walked out,
just like that!'

Judi held the receiver undecidedly in her hand,
then without speaking into it replaced it gently in
its rest. Sarah gaped at her in astonishment.

Having just walked into the house, Judi hadn't
even kicked off her shoes when the phone had been
picked up by her sister. She turned with a sort of
shrug. 'I'm going up to my room. I just
want——'

'If you say you just want to be alone once more
I shall scream!' snapped Sarah, catching her by the
arm. 'Don't you realise he's been on the phone
constantly since the middle of the afternoon?
Mother's been going mad with worry about where
you'd got to, and even Father rang in demanding
to know what's happening!'

'The deal hasn't fallen through, if that's what
he's worried about.'

'You know it's not just that!' scolded Sarah. 'It's
you he's concerned about.'

'Tough.' Judi was too overwrought to be kind.
As she turned the phone burred again, but she pretended not to notice.

'It'll be him,' warned Sarah, glancing at the receiver. 'I'm absolutely not picking it up for you
now you're back.'

'Don't, then. I don't give a damn.'

'It might be Father again.'

Judi gave a shrug and walked out, shutting the
door so that she wouldn't have to hear the sound
that told her Tine was upset to find she had a mind

of her own. She would explain to her father later.
He wouldn't be angry when he learned that everything was still on.

A few minutes later Sarah came into her room.
She didn't knock, and when she entered Judi could
see that her usually easygoing nature had reached
its limit. 'I did in fact speak to him for you . . . and
he says he's got to go back to New York tonight.
I've taken down the numbers he gave me, just in
case you can't lay your hands on them.' She was
obviously quoting Tine himself. 'The first one's his
London number—you can ring no later than seven
p.m. The other one is his private number in
Manhattan.'

Judi took the piece of paper she held out and
tore it into little scraps. 'I'm not ungrateful, Sarah.
I just don't want temptation lying around.' When
she saw Sarah's face she felt contrite. 'I'm sorry—
I will explain, but not yet. It's too—too complex.
Trust me.'

'I don't understand you. What happened today?'

Judi gave a helpless smile. 'Nothing. Precisely
nothing.'

Her sister bit her lip. 'Can't I help?'

Judi shook her head. 'I'm still feeling the after-
effects of living on a desert island. It'll wear off.'

'You're different...' Sarah hesitated. 'Is it simply
that you're finding it difficult to readjust, or is there
something else?'

Judi tried a smile that didn't quite make it.
'Everything's confusing, that's all.'

Sarah said, 'I'm worried about you, Judi. I want
to help, but you don't seem to want to let anyone
near.' She turned away. 'I'm sorry, I'm beginning

to pressure you. Everybody says to give you time to get over things. You've had an awful experience, and I think you're being very brave trying to carry on straight away like this. I'd crack up completely if I had to go through what you've been through.' She paused at the door. 'Is there anything I can get you?'

Judi gave a wan smile. 'You are sweet, Sarah, but no. I just——' she gave a brittle laugh, '—I just want to be alone.'

Still frowning, Sarah went out. Judi rubbed her forehead and gave a sigh. Sarah's concern was almost as annoying as her parents' attitude of sublime patience. She knew they were all watching her for some reason, as if they expected her to crack up or something. But there was nothing to worry about. She was fine, just fine. All she wanted was time on her own. She didn't want fuss—couldn't they see that? There were things to be thought through, and now it looked as if she would have to work everything out on her own.

And as for her father, he would have to send someone else to New York. *She* couldn't do it.

It was not as easy as that. When her father came home that night he called her into his study, and his expression was stern.

'So?' he demanded without preamble.

Judi knew exactly what he meant.

'It's all right,' she said coolly enough. 'He's going to use us. No problems.'

'So why the hell did I get that phone call from him?'

She feigned surprise.

'Come on, Judi!'

For a split second she imagined Tine as distraught at her absence as she had once seen him on the island when he had thought she'd gone missing. He had taken her into his arms in a fierce hug, an unexpected sob shaken out of him as he held her tight. And she wondered just what he had said to her father this afternoon. But then reality made her see another picture. Cool Tine, voice like ice rattling down the line—that was more realistic on current form. 'Did he ask where I was or something?' she asked. 'What's the fuss about?'

Her father shook his head. 'He simply said there were one or two loose ends to be tied up, but you'd had an urgent engagement and left before he could broach them. He thought you might have been back at the office.'

'And I wasn't.' So he hadn't after all cared a damn that she'd run off without saying goodbye. And he'd saved face too, she registered painfully. Not wanting to admit that she had actually walked out on him. He could have no illusions that that in fact was what she had done.

'What loose ends?' She brought herself back to the present.

'Nothing that can't be discussed in greater detail in New York, he said,' rejoined her father.

'Not with me, though.'

He lifted his head.

'I mean,' Judi felt nervous all of a sudden, 'I mean, honestly, Dad, you don't know what he's like. I think you'd have a better deal if you sent some bright young man. The simple truth is that Tine Daniels doesn't like women—at least, not to

do business with. He's the archetypal male
chauvinist. He was hell on the island, and I should
know.'

'And you're telling me you can't handle him?'

She didn't reply.

'Look, Judi, you realise you're talking non-
sense, don't you?'

She remained silent, at a loss how to answer him.

'You must know you're going to come up against
men like that all the time—men like me, in fact!'
He flashed her a roguish smile which she couldn't
return. 'But the truth is that any man with a spark
of intelligence will soon see you're very capable of
handling the job, very capable indeed.'

'But, Dad——'

'I should be very sorry if I thought you intended
to chicken out. It would prove that I'd been right
all along about keeping you out of business.'

Judi stared glumly at the carpet. He was right—
she didn't even have to think it over. There could
be no escape. If she failed to go through with it
this time the threat was plain: he would never let
her near de Burgh again. She lifted her head. 'If
you think he's a man of intelligence, likely to treat
me as just another of the chaps,' she gave a hollow
laugh, 'then OK,' she shrugged, 'I don't agree with
you. But I'll do my best—for de Burgh.'

'Attagirl!' Her father patted her on the shoulder.
'You just have to learn to ignore trivialities,' he said
as they made their way towards the sitting-room.
'Real obstacles are what you have to face up to,
not these imaginary ones of yours.'

Judi reserved her opinion about her father's in-
terpretation of the situation. He was from an older

generation which saw things differently, and, besides, he didn't have all the facts, but she knew she
was going to have to steel herself for the next oc-
casion on which she would meet Tine face to face.

It would be in a foreign country, among
strangers, and all she would have to see her through
was her will to survive.

By the time the aircraft was circling JFK airport a
few days later Judi had honed her thoughts to the
single matter of the assignment in hand. It helped
now to feel the pulse of New York City beating
with an exciting energy of its own as if to feed some
of its heat and vitality into her bloodstream as she
stepped out into the night, and she felt confident
she could cope with anything Tine cared to throw
at her.

His company had sent a courtesy car for her, and
she let herself be carried along on a roller-coaster
ride through the neon-lit streets of Manhattan with
a thrill of excitement at being back in one of her
favourite cities.

There was a large cluster of flowers waiting for
her in her hotel suite, but when she picked up the
card that accompanied them it said simply 'Tine
Daniels Inc.' in printed black italics with his logo
in gold next to it. No signature, no message. She
told herself she felt nothing. Disappointment would
have been inappropriate.

Although the city was still throbbing in the
distant streets below her window she knew she
should get some sleep in order to be fresh for the
ordeal next day, so, armed with a copy of the files
pertaining to the meeting arranged for ten o'clock,

she showered, then slid beneath the covers.
Expecting to feel herself drifting off as she skimmed
over the familiar pages, she was irritated to discover that sleep would not come. She tried to tell
herself she was glad of the extra time in which to
get all the figures well and truly inside her head,
and was just re-reading the summing up for the
hundredth time when the phone beside her bed
began to flicker.

Without thinking she reached over for it.

'Hi...' came a hauntingly familiar voice. 'Have
you settled in all right? Found everything you
need?'

'Tine! I—yes, thanks.' She got over her initial
shock at hearing his voice, but then found there
was nothing else to say. The initiative was taken
from her at once.

'I'm in the lobby and coming straight up.' There
was a click.

Judi found herself trembling from head to foot.
Was it rage or something else? she wondered as she
sprang out of bed and ran to the door. The lock
was across. She slipped the chain into place, then
leaned with her forehead against the frame, suddenly frozen with indecision. It had been an automatic reaction to spring to tend her defences. Tine's
manner provoked such a reaction, for there had
been no 'may I?' or 'do you mind if?' about his
announcement, merely a stark telling, 'I'm coming
up.' Who did he think he was? What right had he
to come marching into her room at this time of
night?

Judi glanced at the bedside clock. It was half-
past eleven, for goodness' sake! Where had he been

until this time? Why call now? He surely didn't imagine she was going to let him in at this time of
night, did he?

Evidently he did, for suddenly there was a soft
knocking on the door, and without making any sort
of decision she found her fingers grappling with
the latch and inching the door ajar.

They eyed each other over the top of the safety
chain. 'Take it off,' he gave it an impatient jangle.
'I want to talk to you.'

'We have a m-meeting at ten o'clock tomorrow.
Won't that do?' she floundered. She was aware of
a powerful sexual chemistry already, and it seemed
to strip her mind bare. Her body seemed to have a
life of its own, crying out in recognition at what
once it had loved. It had been so long since he had
held her in his arms, and now his glance seemed to
burn over her, sending scudding shivers over every
exposed inch of her. Can he tell how much I long
for him? she wondered, pulling the edges of her
kimono more tightly together.

She stepped back from the door, raising her chin.
'I'm sorry, Tine, it's late. I'd already gone to bed,
as you can see.'

'You're not in England now—this is New York.
Things only start to happen at midnight.'

'Not in my hotel room,' she countered, her heart
thudding almost audibly as she held on to the edge
of the door. Her knuckles were taut beneath the
skin.

Slowly, his blue eyes never leaving her face, Tine
lifted one hand and as lightly as a baby's breath
allowed his fingertips to skim hers where she held
the door. She withdrew her hand. 'Don't!' She felt

her senses swim. The entire universe seemed to have pivoted for a moment on that one tiny contact, touch on touch.

'Let me in,' he insisted.

'I've told you—I'd gone to bed. We're meeting tomorrow. You can say whatever it is you want to say then.'

His eyes were blank. 'Maybe it's in your interest to hear what I have to say before the meeting.'

'What do you mean?' Judi narrowed her glance and tried to forget the devastation he was wreaking on her common sense.

'Let me in,' he persisted, 'and then I'll tell you. I'm not prepared to discuss business while I'm standing on one side of a locked door in a hotel corridor!'

'Is this genuine?'

He frowned.

'I mean . . .'

'What do you mean, Judi? Do you think I'm here because I've got nothing better to do?'

'I'm sure you've got plenty to do at this time of night,' she bit back. Remembering the fiancée, she suddenly realised how stupidly she was behaving. If he said it was business that was exactly what it would be. He had given no intimation that he wanted to resume whatever relationship they had had on the island. Quite the contrary.

'I'm sorry,' she mumbled, 'I'm still a little bit confused by the flight and everything. If it's important you'd better come in.'

She let the door off the chain and he pushed it open at once. 'How do you think I feel?' he demanded, striding inside and closing the door behind him.

As it snapped shut Judi realised what she had done. They were alone. The old fire was sweeping through her. What she was supposed to do next—at least, what her body was telling her to do—was throw herself headlong into his embrace, pouring out all the love that was still there. With her emotions boiling to the surface, she remembered in time that he had lied to her, that his affections belonged elsewhere, that it was over.

She spun unseeingly away, finding herself next to the drinks cabinet, saying over her shoulder, 'What do you mean?' her neutral tones hiding the storm within as she rapidly poured two drinks at random and held one out.

'I mean I've been jetting back and forth across the Atlantic as if I was taking a subway,' he told her. 'Been in one meeting after another.' He gave a rueful grin, reminding her of Dan on the island. Her love. She jerked away and didn't look at him. He said, 'They thought I was dead, but nobody could do anything until the lawyers gave the word. They were having a field day! Lucky I got back when I did while there was still something to come back to.' He scowled. 'Still, you don't care a damn about that.'

She lifted her head, but he was gazing moodily into his drink.

'Everything seems so noisy,' she said helplessly. 'The traffic, people, doors opening and closing. I can't get used to it.'

Tine looked up. 'Come here.'

'What?'

'You heard.' He was standing in the middle of the room but made no move to come towards her.

She said, 'It's different now.'

His blue eyes masked his expression. 'Different?'

'You're called Tine, not Dan.' There was bitterness in her voice at the deceit.

'And you're a business executive and daughter of the chairman of one of the most prestigious financial consultancies in the game. Yes.' He gave an ironic smile, his eyes still cold. 'Apart from that?'

'Stop it! Stop it!' Judi gripped her glass with sudden ferocity. 'You said you wanted to talk business. Do it, then, and get out!'

His face became very still and he stared straight ahead without speaking. She had never seen a face look so arctic, and she remembered what he had said about hysterical women. Probably he was comparing her to the soft-as-honey fiancée. But now she had raised her voice she couldn't stop.

'Why the hell have you forced your way in here?' she demanded. 'It's late, and I'm tired. We have nothing to say to each other that can't be said in the meeting tomorrow.'

Tine said nothing. The very blankness of that ice-cold face goaded her to continue. 'You march in here as if you own the place, demanding to talk. But why? What the hell for? It's typical of your arrogance! You were the same on the island—you think you can do what the hell you like. Everybody else just has to fall in with you. Well, let me tell you, some women may like to have themselves pushed around by you, but I don't! *I won't have it!*'

He raised his head, his eyes so cold that she gave a gasp and for a moment forgot what she had been going to say next. But when she opened her mouth to go on he said with deadly calm, 'Shut up.'

He placed his glass on a table with an air of deliberation, then before she could move he had come two paces towards her and his eyes bored into hers as if he was inside her skull. She gave an involuntary step back, legs bumping against a low table, trapping her as he moved slowly and deliberately towards her. In a flat voice, devoid of any emotion, he said, 'Judi, you'll have whatever I choose to give you, no more, no less. Are you listening?'

When she didn't answer he repeated his question, his tones roughening with the raw edge of some unnamed emotion that sent knife-points of fear into her. 'Are you listening, Judi? Do you hear what I'm saying?'

Something numbed her, making it impossible to reply. Her silence seemed to whip his hidden emotions into some sort of peak, for he came forward and took her jaw in his hand, forcing her face helplessly upwards so that he could look down into her eyes. She felt his glance sear over her lips while his own scarcely moved as he said, 'Back in London you made me an offer I can't refuse. You asked me to use you. And that's exactly what I'm going to do...'

CHAPTER NINE

His grip tightened and Judi began to struggle. Neither of them spoke, but the air was rent by the jagged panting of her breath as she fought and kicked to get away. Tine brought the full weight of his muscular body pressing against her own so that she fell back against a cupboard, scrabbling at it behind her back for support before managing to side-step, evading his grasp. But he followed, moving as one with her, both hands tightening around her waist as she reached for safety and jerking her back in an enveloping embrace so that she could feel his hot breath against the back of her neck. Her nightdress gaped as he brought both hands up to cover her breasts. For a moment she swayed against him, head flung back as his lips covered her throat, then she felt a nudge against the back of her knees that sent her crumpling to the carpet at his feet in a billow of cotton and lace.

She was sobbing with a mixture of rage and shock as she reached up to beg silently for release. But still neither of them spoke. What rent the air was Tine's own breath now, rasping in and out with more than mere physical exertion as he bent to her. She had never seen him like this before, single-minded, oblivious to her protests, his face wearing a dead expression as if some secret battle raged within and this physical attack was merely its outward show. She felt his fingers rake through her hair as he tried to drag her beneath him. They were spreadeagled full length now, and she was conscious of a small rug bunched under her where their struggles had pushed it, his hard body pressing down on her.

'Why are you doing this?' she panted when she freed her mouth long enough from his lips to frame the words. His full weight held her a prisoner despite her struggles.

He gave a muffled laugh, his lips twisting, 'You walked out on me the other day!'

'Yes, I did!' she replied heatedly between gasps as he forced her head back on to the carpet.

He gazed down at her like a conquering warlord. Her cheeks were flushed and her sleek hair a mess. She was helpless and he knew it. 'Nobody walks out on me—least of all you,' he intoned, harsh-voiced.

'What do you mean?' Judi managed to croak.

'Shut up!' Before she could protest he brought his lips hard down over her own, covering them so completely she began to squirm with renewed vigour in order to gasp in lungfuls of oxygen, but he didn't seem to notice. She could feel the rug bunch up even more, hurting her back. He didn't care. He didn't give a damn. All he wants, she thought furiously, is to humiliate me, to show who's boss.

His kisses were savage, deep and powerful, giving her no time to recover her senses before they started elsewhere, first moving over her swollen mouth, then to her breasts, fevered and demanding, the dark side to the tender loving they had shared on the island. He seemed to hate her, she thought, to enjoy her helplessness, one hand ripping aside her nightgown, making it gape open to the thigh so that she was revealed in all her nakedness. She struggled helplessly with her knees trussed in the folds of cotton and lace.

'Please don't, Dan, please——' she groaned as she felt his familiar touch begin its explorations of her secret self.

'So it's Dan, is it?'

She didn't reply. Could he tell how much under his command she became when he touched her like that? She tried to brace herself against his mastery, arching to get away, eyes closed tight so she would not have to look at that once much loved face, so that she would not have to witness the blind sexual hunger in it now.

With a ricochet of pure desperation she raised her hips, straining to set herself free from his grasp, but he forced her back, wedging himself across her silvery nakedness, one knee forcing her legs wide, with a savage drawing back of his lips. 'You told me loud and clear what you were like when we were on the island,' he grunted. 'I was a fool to forget those golden words. But it's all right by me. It's not too late to play your game. And a deal's a deal.'

When she managed to gasp a breath she whispered, 'I don't know what you're talking about. What words? What deal?'

'Forget it. Just give me what I want. Come on, baby—you've struggled long enough to whet my appetite. Let's get down to business.'

'Don't you dare touch me——' she began helplessly. She was agonisingly aware that his lips were drawing from her all resistance because they were what she had longed for ever since the rescue, but the way in which he was touching her made her recoil from them now. It was bad enough that he was touching her at all with his faithless hands when he was supposed to be engaged to someone else. 'Don't touch me, you monster!' she cried out. 'How can you?'

'Why not?' he grunted. 'You're irresistible. And you did promise.'

'What about your fiancée?' she managed to stammer, twisting her head this way and that in an effort to avoid his lips.

'You got that from the papers, I suppose?' He gave a dark laugh. 'They rather jumped the gun there. I'm not so easily tied down.'

Judi felt a strange shiver of relief, but also a simultaneous crumbling of her defences. 'Get your hands off me anyway,' she muttered when her lips were freed again. 'Don't touch me... There is no deal,' she added, twisting away.

'You can't renege. It's why you're here, and in London you made it quite clear what you were offering. Anything to further your brilliant career. You offered yourself quite blatantly in return for my company's business.'

'I did not!' She was so shocked that her glance flew to his at once, imagining it must be some kind of joke, but his expression told her he was deadly serious. 'Is that why you said there'd be no obstacles when you rang Father that afternoon?' she asked in astonishment.

'A deal was struck—you set it up yourself. I can only assume it's because you still have a yen for me. Or is this how you intend to do business all through your career?' Tine gave a hollow laugh. 'Why not? Anything goes!'

'You're hateful! How can you say things like this?' Her eyes glistened.

'Quite easily—I know you. Don't forget we spent some very pleasant moments together on Paradise Isle. Sun, sea and sex. You did it to survive then as well. You're a survivor—I should have realised the minute I dragged you out of the water.'

The word paradise had cut her to the soul more even than anything else he was saying. She had used the word often to herself to describe what it was like on the island with Dan. But to hear him—or rather Tine—use the word in that cruel tone made her break inside. She felt a spasm of pain that nearly doubled her, and for a split second the blue eyes showed alarm, but when it happened again he lifted her by the shoulders to a half-sitting position and gave her a disparaging glance. 'Have you been drinking?' he asked roughly.

'It's not that——' she gasped. How could she tell him what he should know when he had no feelings left for her? 'It's just that it makes me feel ill to hear you talk of paradise——' she managed to gasp.

'Very convincing,' he derided, reaching down again to take her breasts. 'Don't forget you called it Hell Isle—both in the papers and when we were there.' He raised his head, blue eyes glazed with sexual hunger, but smiling coldly for a moment as he said, 'That was a good interview you did.' He bent his head again, then lifted it to give her a glacial look. 'I suppose you enjoyed putting the knife into my reputation? Luckily I'm adept at salvaging what I want from the debris, and my press officer is one of the best in the business——'

'Oh, she would be!' Judi tried to drag herself from underneath him, but he jerked her back.

'I haven't finished with you yet. That was only the preliminary skirmish. You should know me better by now.'

'I don't know you—I never have. I know nothing about you except that I hate you and wish we'd never met——'

There was a look of boredom on his handsome face. 'I've heard this before, remember? Can't you tell me something new?'

'Some story, you mean? Like the one you told me?'

'That's rich, coming from you! Runaway heiress in love island paradise. You never breathed a word about that—the heiress bit. But you've had a lot of mileage out of me. Now it's time to collect.'

Judi jerked her head from under his marauding lips and hissed, 'You didn't even tell me your real name! So don't talk to me about stories!'

'My name wasn't relevant.'

'No, because you thought I was after a rich husband!'

'As it was,' he lashed, 'I needn't have worried. You'd have been after me anyway.'

'Your conceit is contemptible! I really hate you!'

'I know. It's your favourite theme.'

'You twist everything!' she went on helplessly. 'You deceived me from the beginning.'

'So did you. Kiss Doran, DJ—one of my employees, no less. Ha!'

'So? I didn't know you were the big boss man in person. And anyway, is that an excuse for not telling me who you were?'

'You know why it had to be like that——'

'Because you thought I was a fortune-hunter and you couldn't see me as anything else, and you wanted to make sure I didn't get my claws into you——'

'And you didn't deny it when I suggested as much.' He gave her a triumphant glance.

Judi looked away. It was true. But she replied, 'Why should I have?'

'Why shouldn't you, if it wasn't true?'

'You know now it wasn't true.'

'I do indeed. Now I know you'd have given yourself like that to any man.' Tine began to laugh with a cynicism that froze her to the roots of her hair. 'Don't worry, baby,' he went on, deliberately lowering his voice to a seductive drawl, 'I'm not blaming you. It was only human nature, wasn't it? Two of us, male, female, naked and alone on a desert island. I'm not blaming you, honey, believe me. You made it all bearable. What more can any red-blooded male desire than a gorgeous body and a beautiful face?' He ran his hands over the body and lowered his mouth towards the face.

Judi lay as if turned to stone. Her worst nightmares were true. None of it, not one solitary moment on that island, had meant anything to him beyond the most crude and basic sexual desire. Oh, but how she loved him! Had loved him. Even now she knew she could love him again. If only, if only fortune, fate would show the way. Her eyes brimmed with tears of desolation, but she fought them back. Never would Tine see her cry again. She had shed all the tears she was going to, and now she was an empty husk. Nothing mattered any more.

'I was wrong about the husband-hunting,' he murmured as he began to feed his desire on her naked flesh, 'if that's what you'd been after you'd have stayed at home. I gather there are plenty of suitable men where you come from.'

'Plenty,' she croaked in agreement. Let him think what he liked. Anything better than the humiliating truth—that she had actually fallen for him, lies and all, and was so spineless that it would take only one gesture for her to throw herself at his feet and let him do with her whatever he wanted.

Full of self-hatred, she remembered how she had imagined him in childhood, the deprived background, knowing now it was a myth, that he had enjoyed as many privileges as she had, and she knew there had been girlfriends a-plenty for him, just as there had been boyfriends for her. There would have been many girls among whom he could pick and choose to find the perfect wife. He was the type to regard it as his hereditary right. And she remembered the girl in the pages of the magazines, smiling up at him, a ring, his ring, on her finger, and the stories the journalists had written about her. And she wondered if she was crying into her pillow at this moment because Tine, callous to the last, had extricated himself when the prospect of serious commitment had arisen.

'None of that matters now,' she muttered in a foggy voice. He was touching her in such a way that she couldn't tell black from white. He turned her thoughts upside down. Her eyes were still glazed, but she opened them and looked straight into his. 'You're right in some ways,' she said huskily. 'We had a wonderful time—the envy of everyone. Why spoil it with all this quarrelling?' With a breaking heart she went on, 'We could pretend we're on the island again—for a few hours, anyway. I don't know why we have to fight... Let's play "let's pretend" like we used to.'

He lifted his head for a moment and she saw him reach out to turn down the lamp. 'Are we staying on the floor?' he asked.

'Why not?' Judi rolled over, untangling her legs from the folds of her gown and kicking free of it so that she was as naked as the goddess of Moon Cove. She rose up and held out her hands, watching as his eyes fastened avidly on her glowing form.

He reached out and wrapped his arms around her waist, burying his face in her soft flesh. She slid slowly down to the carpet and he took her into his arms with a gasp of pleasure, for an instant his eyes widening with a look she hadn't seen all night. Then he jerked his head as if remembering where he was and gave an ironic laugh. 'One thing, darling,' he said in his hard, metallic tones, 'no one can ever accuse us of going to bed together.'

As he enveloped her within his familiar embrace, the one that made her feel there was such a thing as love after all, she told herself he had said that because it would square things should any interested female ask him where he'd spent the night. Verbal niceties would mean a lot to a faithless devil like Tine Daniels.

Then she became mindless in his arms, a pulsing being of pleasure, all the pain of being apart dissolving as they came together in a sweetness of lovemaking that was all the more so because it seemed doomed to end so very soon. One night, she thought. This is all we have. Given Tine's coldness, his lack of real love, she knew that whatever they had could never last. Now she couldn't resist him, but later, surely, she would cease to crave his touch. They were passing strangers now—not friends, but lovers. Together for one night. Soon to be strangers again.

Tine left her side some time in the early hours. As the door clicked behind him after his brief farewell embrace, Judi listened dispassionately to the still constant hum of traffic far below in the dark canyons of the city. She felt unlike herself, dispossessed somehow, as if he had stolen something vital from deep within her. During their night of love she had felt such tenderness for him and such a joy at the secret she longed to share with him that she had almost spoken the words that would have changed things, words that might in the end have given her the appearance of having obtained what she desired above all else—but in reality would have presented her with the mere shell, the trappings of the true love she wanted, without the substance.

For Tine could not love. This she saw clearly now. For how else could he treat her like this? She relived the moment when they had first observed the rescue ship on the horizon, the way his whole demeanour had changed. She recalled the moments after that, the anxious moments, when they were

uncertain whether they had been seen or not. And
then she remembered the joy and excitement in his
eyes as they stepped on board the lighter that was
to take them to the safety of the tanker.

How can he just walk away from paradise? she
had asked herself at the time. The answer was plain
now. It had been nothing to him. It had been as
easy to leave as yesterday's love, which in fact was
what it now was.

His desire tonight had been unmistakable, but
that was easy to understand too. He didn't like to
think she remained immune to him. That she had
used him in order to ensure her survival. Whether
he really believed she had intended to barter herself
for a contract with his company she didn't know.
It was a monstrous thing to think, and she would
have thought he would have known better than to
believe something like that about her. But on the
other hand, he still believed she was just a good-
time girl, with loose morals and a flip, superficial
attitude to life and love.

His bad opinion of her was a wound, but it was
the least of her concerns just now. Feeling the in-
creasingly familiar nausea, she dragged herself off
the bed and went into the bathroom, where she was
neatly and noiselessly sick.

It was dawn already. Grimacing, Judi ran a
shower. Ahead lay the meeting with the board of
directors. She wondered if she would muff things
after a night without sleep. But then Tine had been
sleepless too. They were equals in that.

With the hot water pulsing over her skin she tried
to ease her thoughts back into the familiar mould
where they belonged, the one that set goals and or-

dered her decisions so that she achieved them. Today she had much to prove in the way of determination. She wondered if she had undermined her will by giving in to him last night. But she had wanted him, yearned for him as insatiably as he had seemed to yearn for her. Their bodies did not lie. Whatever Tine thought about her, she knew that truth was when their two physical selves met, and worshipped, and loved each other in unfeigned adoration.

The cab ride to the skyscraper headquarters of Tine Daniels's empire was over quickly, and Judi found herself being catapulted to the penthouse suite where Tine presided like a malevolent black spider in a complex web of deals and contracts.

Awestruck by the aggressively chic edifice of black and silver from which Tine ran things, she forced herself to look thoroughly composed by the time she was ushered in to see him.

He was visible over yards of gleaming ebony desk space, rising to greet the navy-blue-suited figure that stood in the doorway, both of them, she noted, dishonestly alert, as if they had never missed a wink of sleep.

'Judi—on time!' He gave her a distant smile as if the night had never happened. An immaculate secretary or two hovered at his side. 'Let me offer you coffee?'

'I breakfasted at the hotel, thanks.'

He gave a curt nod. 'I'll get someone to show you your office,' he said.

Not moving from the doorway, Judi frowned. 'I'm sure I shan't need to use an office. I've got everything here.' She patted her briefcase.

'No doubt you've got your instructions from your father,' he soothed, 'but I'm sure you'll be wanting to report back before you present your final recommendations later this week——' He paused, giving her time to react to what he was saying.

'Later this week?' she repeated, narrowing her eyes.

'The full board will be meeting on Friday, and no decision can be ratified until then.' He jerked his head with irritation, but she knew he was faking.

She shook her own head. 'I expected to make a presentation today and be back in London tomorrow.'

Tine laughed aloud, a false sound. 'There's no reason for such an unseemly rush, is there?' His expression became glacial when he noticed her obstinate stance, and again she was aware of how formidable he could be in opposition.

'I'm sorry, I hadn't intended to stay so long.'

The secretaries were suddenly discreetly absent, and Judi first realised they were alone when he stood up and came towards her. 'You have to get back for someone special?' he asked.

Their eyes met. He sounded casual. It was the sort of idle question an acquaintance might ask.

'It's none of your concern,' she said in an undertone as one of the secretaries returned.

Tine came right over to her. 'Who is it? The guy you ran away from?' His voice roughened, but in the same undertone he demanded, 'He's still around?'

A way of saving face seemed to leap out at her. 'Certainly.' She looked up, giving him a wide, false smile. 'He's always around. Almost part of the family.' It was true, except that it happened to be Sarah he came to see every day and not herself. Something made her add, 'Patrick happens to be the faithful type.'

'I take it that's a gibe at me?' he went on in the same tone. 'I can't imagine why. I'm quite capable of being faithful to the right woman.'

'It's just that you haven't found her yet,' she finished for him. Her eyebrows rose. 'This fiancée didn't last long.'

'Nothing in the daily papers ever does. You know how the Press always put a slant on things.'

The secretaries came back again, together with a couple of executives in dark suits who made across the steel-grey carpet towards them.

'A slant? Do they?' Judi's voice was discreet, but the irony in it was unmistakable.

'Don't they?' Tine persisted, glancing over his shoulder.

'If you say so.'

They glared at each other, his hostility all at once apparent beneath the civilised veneer of his earlier manner.

'I don't know why you have to make these barbed remarks,' she said quickly in an undertone. 'Fate threw us together as some kind of cosmic joke and now we're apart again, each where we belong. I accept that.'

'The spheres in their orbits, turning, turning...' His face was like a stone mask.

Judi felt her fingers tighten convulsively on her briefcase. It was Dan speaking. But he was a figure from the past. He had no place in the here and now. She couldn't cope. Her heart wouldn't take any more. With a flippant jerk of her shoulders she said, 'The past is past—as you said.'

Then she turned. The older of the two men had been hovering just out of earshot, but now he stepped forward, extending a hand. All through the introductions she was aware of Tine's soulless blue eyes boring into her, and it made her nerves jump. In a second I'm going to do something totally out of line, she thought with a tremor. It made her more determined than ever to preserve a nerve of steel.

After the meeting she went to the ladies' and was quietly sick again. Apart from that, everything had gone brilliantly within the limits Tine had prescribed, and it was obvious the final decision would go in her father's favour. In the circumstances Judi had capitulated on the matter of an office, only momentarily dismayed to discover that it was a pleasant ante-room in Tine's own personal suite.

The thought of having to spend a few days in proximity to him made her quake with trepidation. She doubted whether her self-control could hold out so long. And what about the night? What if he came to her room again? Would she give way as easily as she had done last night? He had said he would use her, and that was exactly what it amounted to.

A call to her father put him in the picture so far as the assignment went and he seemed unperturbed by the fact that she was having to stay on. She told him everyone was extremely enthusiastic. Tine, she said, had made a point of saying how pleased he was with the way things were going. At the time she had suspected he meant something else by this remark, but she passed it on anyway. She was in a storm of confusion. Only her feelings for Tine and the knowledge that he didn't return them stood out clearly.

She was running over the events of the day and jotting down a few notes in her day book when there was a sound behind the half-open door of her office.

She looked up from her desk.

He was here again.

And the way he kicked the office door closed behind him told her that the building was empty.

Tall, dark and dangerous, fully at ease as he strode into her room, he repossessed it—repossessed her—with that smile of his that didn't quite reach the glacial blue of his eyes. He didn't pause but bulldozed straight across the room, reaching out for her, leaning over her desk, placing one hand on each of her shoulders and holding her transfixed. His captive.

Judi could feel his fingers pressing possessively against her, their heat palpable through the thin wool of her cashmere sweater. It was as if he had a right to touch her.

She felt a tremor of desire quake through her. She wanted to resist him and he knew it, but just as surely one look told her he wasn't going to take no from her.

'It's late,' she stalled in a shaky voice, stuck rigidly to her chair. 'I was just about to go back to my hotel to change for dinner...'

'I think not.' He moved sleekly round the desk towards her. 'Not yet,' he breathed. 'You have an account to settle. Surely you don't imagine I'd be satisfied with that one night?'

She had to lean back in order to look up at him, the angle of her head making her feel defenceless. But she tried to bring some order to her thoughts. 'You made up your mind this morning that you were going to make me stay over for a few days, didn't you?' she challenged.

Unabashed, Tine gave a brief nod. 'Of course I did. It seemed the only solution.'

'Why, Tine, why?' Her eyes were fixed on his and she gripped the edge of the desk, but otherwise she couldn't move to escape.

'I told you the reason,' he said, in that throaty drawl that made her knees buckle with the foreknowledge of what he could make her do.

'Because I stupidly made some remark about being glad for you to use me?' She dared not look at him now. She felt trapped. He wanted her, he would have her. She wanted it to happen. But she hated him, and she hated herself for being driven to something dangerous and beyond control again like last night. 'When I said you could use me I meant the company, our services—you know I did!'

He laughed harshly. 'Does it matter? It comes to the same thing. If you're going to survive in this dirty game you're going to have to use every advantage you've got.'

'Never sex. Never that, Tine. I couldn't live with that.'

In reply he merely smiled in such a way that she felt a curl of fear travel slowly up her spine. Would he insist if he knew how much she loved him? If he knew the secret she was hiding? She half turned her head, hoping he would have second thoughts, but she felt him reach for her, the seductive assault of his presence making her head swim for a moment, then she was shivering uncontrollably as she felt his fingers sliding slowly down the back of her neck. In another moment he had pulled her to her feet and she was engulfed in his arms, her face pressed up hard against the rough material of his jacket. She felt his lips against her temples, then they began to slide slowly over her eyes, effectively closing them so that she became more vibrantly aware of the scent and texture of him, his body heat, the palpable energy of his desire. He began to insert his fingers inside the waistband of her sweater, lifting it inch by inch as his lips drained all resistance from her. Then he looked down.

When he saw her breasts, naked beneath oyster silk, Tine paused for a second and she saw his tongue dart quickly over dry lips as his eyes glazed and his dark head came down in a sensual taking of her breasts that sent her arching in a convulsion of pleasure before she could stop herself.

'No——!' she cried brokenly. 'Not again... please, Tine, and not here...'

'Again, Judi. Again and again until we've exhausted our desire. Come to me, give me your mouth.' He held the sides of her head, keeping her face still, dipping repeatedly to rake his lips abrasively over hers.

'Somebody might come in...' she tried to protest, but he was deaf to her objections.

'Now,' he murmured. 'I want you. I want you now...'

Something seemed to have taken hold of him, driving him on into some wordless region where common sense, propriety, convention no longer existed. 'I want to drown in your body,' he said hoarsely. 'Give yourself to me, Judi. Don't hold back. Give me everything...'

CHAPTER TEN

THERE was a lull before Tine brought his head down to cover her mouth with his own again. Then he lifted his head, his eyes raking her face. Judi was scarcely breathing, and she flinched as he gave her an unemotional examination. Both of them seemed poised as if hesitating before plunging over the edge into the abyss.

Now that his words had tailed away he was gazing at her as if trying to see into her mind, and her attention sharpened and she became aware of the faint hum of the air-conditioning and the office opening out emptily beyond this one. On the other side of the fishbowl-windows she was aware of the backdrop of clouds with other skyscraping top-floor offices shining distant and small against the night. With no prospect of help from any quarter she realised she must find some strength of resistance within herself.

'Tine,' she began in a shaky voice, clearing her throat when it came out as a croak, 'you do realise this is wrong? I don't want you. I'm saying no.'

He gave a dismissive laugh, but she went on, 'If you insist, I shall have you in a court of law as quick as that——' She tried to snap the fingers of one hand, but it didn't quite come off. The other was supporting her trembling body against the edge of the desk behind her back. She could feel it digging into her thighs as she tried to widen the gap

between them both. She shifted, straightening a
little, trying to outface him.

'Law?' he breathed. 'You'd go to law because I
made love to you?' He laughed. 'I suppose you
could do that,' he went on in his dark velvet tones,
'but will you?' He bent to take her more possessively into his embrace.

He didn't give a damn, she saw. He wasn't taking
her threats seriously at all. Her lips tightened. 'Try
it,' she clipped, anger giving her strength. 'Just try
it! Let's see how good it's going to look splashed
all over the papers. See if your press officer can
talk her way out of that one for you!'

'It would be worth the risk,' he murmured, blue
eyes lingering over her face. 'But I don't think you'd
do a thing like that. You wouldn't have the face to
stand up and deny that you wanted me. You know
you'd never get away with it.'

'I would! So I would!' Her pale face flushed with
anger. 'Try me!'

'But I would merely tell them how you offered
yourself. How I couldn't resist. Afterwards you
were moved by a spirit of revenge!' Tine was
laughing softly, playing with her, knowing she had
no arguments to marshal against him. She was self-
consciously aware that he guessed that the flush on
her cheeks and the brightness of her eyes were because of the battle warring within her now.

'I'd get the best lawyers available,' she went on
breathlessly. 'You'd never get away with it.'

'There would have to be signs of struggle,' he
countered. 'Bruises, cuts, torn clothing——' He
began to touch her breasts in a way that made her
long to capitulate, to touch him in return, but in

love, not like this, with what was lustful and
without true feeling.

'There will be all that,' she countered, trying to
steady her swimming senses. 'There'll be evidence
that you'd made me—forced me to make love
against my wishes.'

'Evidence? You mean you'll fight me? Now?
You'll show how violently you're resisting me?' He
placed one hand on the other side of her on the
desk, locking her in, and now he raised the other
hand and lightly skimmed her lips with his fingertips. 'Are you resisting me?' he asked, and when
she didn't answer, couldn't answer, he said in a soft
voice that made her insides melt, 'I've smeared your
lipstick. Let me wipe it off for you.'

'No, don't——!' Judi averted her head, but he
produced a handkerchief, and though she shook her
head from side to side she was forced to suffer
having her lips thoroughly wiped. It made her feel
as helpless as a child, somehow enfeebling her resistance. The fine white linen was streaked with
scarlet rose, like blood, like defeat.

'And your hair,' he went on, still soft-voiced, his
eyes lasering over her upturned face, 'it would have
to look a little dishevelled, wouldn't it? Not this
hard, glossy cap as if it's never been touched. It
looks untouched . . . untouched.' As he spoke he let
the soiled handkerchief drop to the floor and
brought up one hand to her hair, running his fingers
rapidly through it until she knew it was as wild as
in the days when he had twined flowers in it. The
image made her heart miss a beat.

'Don't, Tine,' she said brokenly. 'I have to go
back to the hotel—now, at once. Please . . .'

'Not yet, not yet,' he murmured as he pressed his face against the side of her head. 'We have something to do first. You promised—you owe me. You can't back out.'

His voice hardened and she knew she couldn't argue with him and win. And she knew she couldn't fight and win. But she clung to one last hope that if there were signs of physical resistance he would think twice about what he had in mind and his common sense would save her.

'You don't believe I'm saying no,' she managed to whisper as she began to struggle, 'but I am!' She pushed at his hands, striking out, hitting at the side of his face, but afraid to use any really effective means of self-defence in case she hurt him. As her hands pummelled uselessly against his chest she knew she couldn't help pulling punches, would rather he did make love to her than that she should ever hurt him. With a sudden sob she capitulated, crumpling against him, feeling him catch her strongly in both arms and hold her hard against him. She felt the desire to be held and held forever by him sweep her on, but there still remained a shred of pride, a remnant of the will to resist.

She raised her head. 'I hate you, Tine, I hate you! I don't want you. Why should you think I do?' Her face felt hot, but she tried to give him a look severe enough to convey the strength of her resistance, and for a moment their glances locked in stark hostility before Judi felt her own slide away to conceal the upswing of love that could not be hidden.

His fingers slid beneath her chin, tilting her face, positioning her lips for the taking, his other hand vicelike at the back of her head, his hard, male body coming crushingly against her own, pressing her back against the edge of the desk, forcing her body to release a sudden wild plunge of desire.

'I'm going to do this without giving you a single bruise, without tearing off a single button,' he told her in a voice suddenly hoarse with a hunter's excitement. 'Resist me, Judi, resist now while you have the chance, and let me teach you what I mean.' As he spoke he slipped her sweater over her head before she could prevent him, and she heard the zip on her navy blue skirt slide down.

'No!' she protested. Her long fingers clawed at his collar as he began to bring his lips little by little to within an inch of her own. She was breathing in the scent of him, the familiar hot, secret chemistry that dizzied her senses and turned her world inside out, and her limbs were beginning to tremble with the need to learn him again and again. She was empty without him, a husk. Even with the secret she carried, that part of him she would have forever, she felt empty without him. Her head tilted defensively, her neck revealing all its fragile length along which his lips began to trail in endless pursuit as if he was seeking some mystery of union not only of their two bodies but of something deeper and hidden and powerful beyond themselves.

Now he had stripped her of her garments she stood defenceless in only her stockings and bra, and she felt herself opening helplessly to his touch, his mastery, her body swaying like a flower, and she knew they approached something as deep as life itself and as unstoppable.

'Tine——'!' she husked as if the knowledge of it wounded her. 'Please don't, please, I beg of you...' But her fingers lost themselves in the endless pleasure of his hair and he murmured throatily, 'I don't call this fighting back.'

'Please don't...' she moaned against the side of his head.

'You want me. Just say it!'

'No, no!' she whispered in a turmoil of desire.

'You can't stop now, Judi,' he rasped. 'You know it!'

'Take me, then,' she whimpered in a fever of longing as she felt her body's betraying response when he peeled away the last of her garments, 'take me, take me... let's love each other as we did on Paradise Isle...'

A groan of assent was wrested from him and in a voice like black velvet, the one that had first brought her into his world, he told her, 'We're in Moon Cove on the beach, ocean on all sides, night coming down...' With a convulsion that snatched her up into his arms again he seemed to turn her body to wax, moulding it around himself, coming into her melting heat with a fierce masculine fire of his own, hurting her with an extremity of pleasure that made her mindless with giving.

Now the night was filled with the sounds of love, their two shadows as one against the wall behind the desk, while beyond the fishbowl-glass the night sky and the great city stretched around them as limitless as the ocean of their imaginations, and the black and silver bower in the sky became a time-capsule carrying them back to when they had loved without pretence.

It was at the swiftly attained height of ecstasy that both cried out in love, a mingling of two voices, a brief sharing. A moment later Judi felt a fountain of salt water springing from her eyes. It was soundless, sending shudders of release through her to match the receding love tremors, and it made Tine hold her close, hard, tight, hurting her, as if to stop any breach between them. Then slowly the waves receded, calm lapped over them, the only sound a rhythmic breathing established in unison, the shape on the wall shifting, separating, vanishing as Tine at last stood back. His voice shook. He said, 'I didn't mean to make you cry.'

Wordlessly Judi gazed back at him from her position among the mangled files and papers on her desk, wondering if the office looked as she felt, as if a tornado had hit it. She blinked away the salt in confusion, unable to pick and choose among the many words jostling to be spoken out loud. Tine held her glance, an ambiguous expression on his face as if to ask, did this really happen to us? It was as if something else had taken over.

She gave a shudder. Sprawling like this where he had abandoned her, there could be no pretence that this was Paradise Island.

When he pulled on his shirt she self-consciously slid to her feet, the deep carpet coming as a shock against her bare soles. Averting her face, she reached hurriedly for her own clothing, pulling things on anyhow. Recriminations were beginning to swarm into her mind. She was crazy about him. But what had come over her—here? How could she have so far forgotten common sense and propriety? What if someone had come in? She had been as oblivious as Tine had to the possibility, swept along by some madness of desire. She swayed, the navy blue skirt clutched protectively in one hand as if to conceal herself from his inevitable contempt.

She heard the rasp of fabric as he pulled on his clothes, then she stepped into her slip and dragged the cashmere sweater over her head before having the nerve to speak. Her lips were trembling. 'I assume you do this sort of thing all the time,' she clipped, not daring to look at him.

There was a telling silence from across the room, and she risked a glance. Tine was buttoning up his shirt, but his fingers came to a stop when she spoke and now he was staring at her, his face an enigmatic mask, his blue eyes depthless and without emotion.

She shuddered at the arctic sweep of them, chilled to the soul. What action did pride demand now when all of it was lost? What was the sophisticated thing to do? She felt gauche, cheap, used, in utter despair—love was only a word in a popular song. Nothing meant anything. She had given everything to Tine, had not been able to resist because of this inconsolable love which he held in contempt. Now they were picking up their clothes from the carpet separately, like two strangers. Why had he treated her like this, and why had she allowed it? She was beyond tears.

Rapidly zipping up her skirt, she pulled on her smart businesswoman's jacket, smoothed back the dark bob, flicking a glance at him as he finished buttoning up his shirt. She watched him pull on his jacket and finally roll up his tie and put it in his pocket.

When he was ready he gave her a strange, lingering glance. 'What now?' he said eventually in a flat voice, dropping the words into the space between them like stones.

Judi shrugged. What now? What else could there be? Only one thing. Goodbye.

Unable to say the word, she simply gazed and gazed at him with wide beseeching eyes, hoping her face was in shadow so that the telltale signs of love in it would not betray her.

'I suppose,' he said, not moving, 'we might have a bite to eat.' He paused. Then he stepped forward, being careful not to touch her. 'Come, I'll take you back to your hotel. We'll eat there.'

Wordlessly Judi straightened the chaos of papers on the desk, tamping everything back into her briefcase with bent head, switching off the desk lamp and straightening the chairs, while Tine stood, all the while silent, silhouetted in the doorway by the light from the outer office.

'That's that, then,' he said when she finished. She gave one last brief glance round the room. There was no sign, no echo, nothing at all, to show that such passion, such wildness had erupted within its well-ordered walls.

Feeling dead and cold inside, she followed him out, watching robot-like as he switched off lights en route to the lift. Then, in a matching of her inner state, he was leading her down, endlessly down to the depths below.

Afterwards she remembered the sound of his footsteps mismatching with hers on the concrete as they crossed the underground car park. She remembered the rich smell of leather upholstery as they belted themselves into his vintage sports car. She dwelt all through the short meal that followed on the sight and sound of him, the dark head turning, turning away from her, his eyes clouded, petrol blue, avoiding hers. She remembered the small talk, the signs that he felt as dismayed by their un-bridledness as she did.

Then they were moving towards the restaurant exit. This it it, she thought. Now we say goodbye. We part. I go to my room—but I shall not cry all night. I shall not cry at all. He will *not* drive me to despair. She remembered the secret life inside her. I have that, she told herself, already turning away towards the lift, turning from Tine before he saw the look in her eyes. As she reached out to draw down the means of escape his hand came over hers, gripped it, lifted it almost to his lips, then stopped, holding it in front of him.

'I'm coming up with you, Judi,' he said.

Taken by surprise, she stepped back. 'There's no need.' Her head jerked. 'I think I can manage to get up to my room by myself——'

'I said I'm coming up.'

For one wild moment she thought he meant he wanted to inflict on her again the loveless love of an hour ago. She felt her cheeks blanch, but he let her hand drop in order to hold back the lift doors. His eyes swept her face. 'We need to talk,' he snapped, then gestured her forward with a rough jerk of his arm.

Almost falling into the lift, Judi did as he ordered. It would be all blame, she knew. A slanging match. If she let go of her self-control all the recriminations she had felt ever since she had read his account of their time together would come flaring out and she would be unable to hold any of it back. All the way up she kept her glance averted, working on her self-control, until by the time they reached the door of her room she was sure she was in charge of it.

Tine marched straight inside with his usual air of ownership and poured them both a drink. When he handed it to her his eyes glittered with an intensity she had never seen before.

'I suppose you feel you've settled the contract to everyone's satisfaction?' he began brutally. 'Well done! I can tell you that whatever my present feelings of distaste your father can rest assured that we'll do business together.'

Before he could go on again Judi stepped forward. 'Wait! Before you say anything else...' she half turned so as not to have to face his arctic expression. '...I should say I've decided to ask him to get someone else to liaise with you in future... It would be better that way.' Her fingers were white on the stem of her glass.

'We need never meet again,' came his voice from behind her. Despite his words it wrapped round her as softly as black velvet. She loved his voice, its every timbre. When it came again she could tell he had moved closer.

'Judi, I'm not in the game of ascribing blame. Whatever my feelings about what happened just now, I was as much to blame as you. It shouldn't have happened.' His voice thickened and she heard him say, 'I didn't want it to be like that, but you drove me to it. I lost control—I shouldn't have, but

I did. And I can't guarantee it won't happen again so long as you're around. It's you, Judi. You turn me into someone I don't know. And I made you cry.'

She couldn't turn, though she longed to witness the look in his eyes. The inflexions in his voice told her nothing, they were so carefully level. Part of her wanted to turn on him, demanding apologies, screaming at him to ask how dared he offload one particle of blame on to her for what had happened. Another part told her she knew that she had wanted him to take her like that, that something wild had driven her to say 'let's love each other' as if the old days could be revived. Tears stung her eyes at the thought of what they had lost.

Sensing that Tine was standing right behind her now, she half turned, her glance coming directly into contact with the front of his shirt. Lifting her chin, she was in time to catch sight of a brooding look that quickly transferred itself into the glacial expression he had worn before.

'For what it's worth, you've proved something to me for a second time,' he said flatly.

Judi's lips tightened a fraction as if she knew what was coming next. More blame, more criticism, a reference to her wantonness, a reminder that he still thought of her as Kiss Doran. She waited.

'No,' he breathed after a lengthy scrutiny of her face, 'nothing like that. That's only the surface. I'm not a fool. Sometimes I can see beneath the glossy image.'

Her lips opened and closed when she failed to select a single phrase from the many that were crowding into her mind.

'What you've proved,' he continued before she could find anything to say, 'is that I never get you right. Where you're concerned I can't think straight. On the island, when things were so frightening for both of us, you were always there, reliable, quick to see what had to be done, even though it was an environment more alien to you than to me. I respected that.' He gave a shrug. 'If that sounds pompous, I'm sorry. I find it difficult to——' he paused, '—well, to say this sort of thing.'

Judi could feel a restriction across her ribs, as if something enormous was being held in. If it was difficult to say, why was he bothering at all? And why hadn't he said all this on the island so that she wouldn't have had to go through such hell? Was he offering it now as some sort of farewell speech? Why didn't he just say goodbye—thanks for the memory?

But he was going on. 'This second time, you presented the case for your company quite brilliantly, despite my hostility. That was another surprise. I thought I was going to have to help you all the way through. I should admit I thought it might be a case of a rich man's daughter being indulged. But you've justified your father's confidence in you. You're good. You're going to be wildly successful in your own right.'

She dropped her glance. The pain in her chest was strangling her words, but she managed to get them out. 'As it happens,' she said slowly, with the idea coming more clearly as she put it into words, 'it's unlikely I shall go on with my career. I think maybe I shall take a year or two out. It's been good to know I can hold my own in a boardroom, and at one time it was all I wanted. But I feel confused now.' She hesitated. 'It's as if something happened on the island to make me change——' She nearly choked, but forced herself to continue. 'My ambitions seem different now. When I got back I began to think about the kind of life I wanted to lead, and I feel it's going to be very different from what I'd imagined in those pre-island days.'

She could have said, in the pre-Dan days, but she didn't have the courage, or the reckless lack of pride. She lifted her head, even managing a tentative smile. 'I'd like to live in the country, somewhere beautiful and challenging.' Somewhere, she was thinking, where a child can run free and learn about the seasons of the year. An image of the future, bleak because it was one in which Dan or Tine would never figure, swam before her eyes.

She turned abruptly and groped her way across the room without waiting to witness his reaction. He let her go, and she found her way into the bathroom, leaning with tear-blind eyes against the washbasin until the pain had eased, then bending swiftly to dash cold water over her face, erasing any signs of the emotion that had printed itself there.

When she returned she was composed, her face pale but unstained, lips red again, her whole appearance glossy and unemotional. Tine looked up as if searching for signs of something, but, apparently not finding anything on which to comment beyond the sight of her scarlet lips, which elicited a brief raising of his eyebrows, he stretched out on the jade-coloured chesterfield and loosened his jacket.

'You won't mind if I spend the night, will you?' he said. 'I'm too dog-tired to drive back home.'

'If I say no I suppose you'll stay anyway,' she said, forcing the words out with a sort of flippancy that amazed her. Their eyes met.

Tine gave an abrupt laugh. 'You only have to say no and mean it,' he paused. 'That's all you've ever had to say.'

He shut his eyes, and she had a chance to study the lines of his profile, memory and desire tugging at her heart and the great loneliness in realising that he would never know how much she loved him almost sending her running to make a confessional of his embrace.

Instead she resisted the impulse and went over to the television, flicked a switch and found a news channel in the hope that it would blot out the howl of pain that was trying to get out. Everything seemed to be cracking up around her—the outside world, her world, the inward one from which all effective action sprang.

When Tine eventually leaned over to turn down the sound she went on gazing uncomprehendingly at the flickering images. All she had seen for the last hour had been Dan, Dan, Dan...

'That's enough of that.' He reached out to her. 'We're not an old married couple with nothing to say to each other.' He leaned towards her. 'It's time for bed, Judi.'

His words were like a lash, and unexpected enough to send her jerking to her feet. What had she expected? she asked herself. Why else would he stay? She felt his eyes upon her as she began to pace back and forth across the carpet. When she turned she was trembling, and the words began to pour out before she could stop them. She said in a harsh voice, 'I know you think I'm made of stone, all lacquer and brittleness and nothing much inside. But I beg of you not to—not to touch me.' Her voice dropped to a whisper on the last two words. Something hot was trickling down her cheeks, but she went on looking at him, beseeching him, wide-eyed, willing him to listen to what she was saying.

He stayed very still and let his glance linger over her, the fists clenched by her sides, the unaccustomed tension obvious in every line of her body as she moved angularly towards him.

'Please, Dan, you're killing me. Can't you see? I know you don't care—why should you?—but I simply can't stand it——' Her pride suddenly deserted her and she was blurting out all her misery, saying, 'When you make love to me and I know you don't give a damn it's like being mutilated. It's as if you're cutting something precious from inside me. I can't, Dan, please don't make me... You know I can't say no to you... I've tried! God, I've tried, but I can't do it. Please have pity... I love you so...'

He was on his feet and reached out for her before she knew what was happening. *'Judi!'*

He wrapped her in his arms and held her for so long without speaking or moving that she could count the syncopations of their heartbeats. He was breathing heavily, the rise and fall of his chest matching her own as she strove for control. Something was beginning to engulf her, a warmth, a tenderness, something she had longed for, but something in which she no longer believed—at least, not as it emanated from Tine Daniels.

He heard her give a stifled sob. It made him bend his head. 'My love, my precious lover! How was I to know you felt like this? I thought you didn't feel anything for me any more. I thought it had all gone.' He stroked her hair just as he had done on the island as she fought her way out of unconsciousness.

His voice was rougher when he spoke again. 'I didn't dare believe it when you said ''let's love each other like we did on the island.'' I thought you meant simply let's make love. But then you cried...' He stroked her cheek. 'After we left the island I began to think you must have been playing at love because you were scared I'd ditch you and you'd have to fend for yourself. Kiss Doran, survivor. There was no other way to account for your coldness when we got back.'

'You *left* me, Dan! You walked off without looking back. When we were rescued you just left me. You didn't even come to the airport. You changed the minute we sighted the ship.'

'Changed? Yes,' he agreed after a moment, 'perhaps I did. My mind was full of all the things I was going to have to face when I got back. But then you changed too. You were so strange, as if you were in another world already—one you didn't want me to share.'

A flicker of rapid emotion made her jerk up her head to gaze into his face as if seeking confirmation that what he was saying was true. '*You* doubted *me*?'

He nodded. 'We were separated by the Press, and by the time I got to the airport to see you off your plane was already disappearing into the night. I seemed to go into some kind of limbo after that— meetings round the clock, jetting back and forth across the Atlantic. And when I rang you you didn't want to know. I was devastated. Then I remembered Kiss Doran, and I felt cheated. I haven't been thinking straight since then, partly because I was unable to adjust to the speed and noise of city life. Half the time I didn't know where the hell I was——'

'You too?' Judi asked, raising her head. Despite the hot salt water soaking her cheeks the pain that was strangling her seemed to ease a little. 'It confused you too?'

'I'm not Superman,' he told her. 'All I wanted was to fly to you, kidnap you back to Love Island and live native ever after. I was in a sort of madness, knowing it was impossible just then. Telling myself that tomorrow, the day after, the next day, then would be the time to let the world go and hold you in my arms again.' He gripped her tightly against him as if he would never let her go now.

'But the interviews?' she whispered, unsure whether it was Dan or Tine talking.

'Is that what made you so hostile? God, I'll sue the lot of them! You didn't believe all that stuff, did you?'

'I felt I didn't really know you after all,' she admitted, shamefaced.

'I told you, the Press always put a slant on things. There was no fiancée, but it was useless telling them that, so they went on printing those ridiculous stories. My press secretary thought it a great joke, especially as her current boyfriend is the laid-back type. It made him sit up all right!'

'I thought you'd lied to me,' she said, moving her fingers over and over through his thick black hair. 'I thought you'd lied. I thought it had all been a fantasy. I didn't know what to do, except fight back the way you'd taught me.'

He was rocking her back and forth, his eyes closed against the side of her head. 'The fantasy is this crazy life of deals and contracts. I want out as soon as I can tie things up. And if you do too...'

'You mean...? I don't understand.'

'When you said you dreamed of a life in the country just now it struck a chord with me. I can never go back to the old life, not after living in paradise.' He held her close. 'It is the same for you as it was then, isn't it? You're my woman, Judi. I can't live without you. The days since we came back have been a nightmare.'

They rocked back and forth and she lifted her lips to touch his jaw. 'I love you so much, Dan. You were everything to me on the island, and you still are.'

'Then if you agree we'll find some land somewhere, build a house, run outward-bound courses for youngsters, turn what we learned about survival to good use and show city kids another way of life. That's my dream, Judi. Will you share it? Oh, my love, say yes!'

'That sounds suspiciously like another order, Tine Daniels,' she replied in a choky voice. She was smiling, tears staining her cheeks but her smile transcending them.

'Yes, it is an order, one you mustn't disobey. But if you want me to plead with you I'll do that too. I'll even go down on my knees for you.' The intensity was replaced by the bright blue glitter of another emotion, and she laughed to see it, astonished when he did indeed drop to his knees. 'Please, lover,' he growled, 'come with me. I need you. I've never needed anyone in my life, but I need you. I want you. Say yes!'

She slid down in front of him. 'Dan, I can't believe this is happening. I've been so unhappy, it was like living in a nightmare. All I wanted was for you to love me. I'll live anywhere, do anything. Just to be with you.'

That night they made love in a bed for the first time in all the long months they had loved each other. And some time in the small hours, as the moon slanted across the sheets, Judi remembered to tell Tine the secret she had held to herself for so long. 'Our baby,' she murmured. 'It was the only thing that kept me sane in the middle of the nightmare of losing you.'

He was sombre. 'And you were going to face that alone?'

She cuddled closer. 'I felt I had to. It would have been no good being together without love.'

He stroked her moon-pearl shoulder and she could feel him looking down at her out of the darkness. 'Never once have you questioned why I kept you at arm's length for so long.' He kissed one of her temples. 'Did you never wonder why I was like that?'

She shook her head. 'I guessed it was because I was Kiss Doran and pretty useless at everything, with those long red fingernails and that little sequinned sarong.' She kissed his bare chest, letting her lips linger over the moon-defined muscles and momentarily losing her train of thought in the pleasure his touch aroused. But then she went on, 'I can understand why you couldn't be bothered with me when you thought I was so dim and useless.'

'Idiot,' he corrected gently. 'It wasn't that at all. You were perfect—a real right hand. I couldn't have done anything without you. And I was crazy about you from the moment I first saw you.'

'Naked in the waves?'

'No, taking strawberries from between another man's fingers. I liked your pep, your style, your beautiful face and endless legs. I wanted you. I didn't sleep that night! But I told myself I couldn't get involved with my customers. Especially one who would turn my life upside down.'

'But why were you so horrible to me on the island, then?' Her eyes opened wide.

'Because I foolishly thought we could avoid making love if I kept you at arm's length. How's that for idiocy?'

'But why would you want to do that? It was the most perfect place for loving, as we discovered!'

'It wouldn't have been perfect if you'd got pregnant and we hadn't been rescued,' Tine told her sombrely. 'And it was just like Kiss Doran not to think of a thing like that.'

Judi snuggled closer to him, wrapping herself tightly round his strong body. 'You're right as always, Dan. I never thought of the consequences until too late. And then, luckily, we were rescued anyway.' She began to kiss him methodically in a way that made him groan with pleasure. 'For perhaps the first time in my life,' she told him as she worked her way over his perfect physique, 'I'm happy to take orders. I wouldn't take them from anyone else, but with you it's different. I worship you. You're so clever. You make everything right.'

'I hope you always think so. I'll never let you down.'

'I know that. I've known it from the very beginning.'

'You have to promise me one thing,' he told her seriously, placing both hands on either side of her head and tilting her face towards him for a moment so that the silver light coming in through the windows illumined her face.

'What's that, my love?'

'Promise that as soon as I can free myself from all my business interests you'll live with me in the wilds somewhere, far away from the noise and confusion of the cities.'

Looking at his face in the moonlight, Judi could only smile lovingly at the thought of their future. 'Of course I will. I promise,' she told him passionately.

'And you won't regret giving up the jet-setting life you could have?'

'As if! I want to live in your so-called wilds, Dan darling, to be with you forever. It sounds like paradise already. Just you, me and the baby, on an island of love.'

*   *   *

The cove was an empty curve of silver sand with the turquoise sea, lace-edged, tamed within the reef. A trail of footprints wove in and out of the water's edge as if the two people they belonged to had made frequent forays into the waves. Tracked to a promontory beyond a group of drooping palms, the owners of the footprints looked back along the beach. They could have been an advert for a tropical paradise, the tall dark-haired handsome man in the dazzling shorts and battered straw hat, the young woman in the sarong, a simple necklet of exotic flowers her only adornment, and the tiny baby, gurgling happily in her father's arms, tugging playfully at the hairs on his bronzed chest.

Then Judi reached out and took the tiny fist in hers. 'Soon,' she said to her husband, 'Danielle will be walking.' She put both arms round her husband's shoulders and he slid his around her hips so that they held the baby between them.

'Next time we come back she'll be swimming,' he told her proudly. They both gazed back at the sheltered waters of the cove. It would be a child's paradise, just as it had been theirs.

'It's such a tiny island, isn't it?' Judi smiled softly into Tine's handsome face. 'Difficult to believe we were here for so long.'

'Even more difficult to believe they ever found us.' He gripped her tightly, careful not to squash Danielle as he placed a kiss on her brow.

One of his helicopters had dropped them on the island for a few hours. With the baby they had no intention of spending the night there, but now Judi was regretful. 'We will come back again, won't we, Tine? For old times' sake. And to show Danielle what a beautiful place Love Island is, the place where she was nearly born!'

'Every year,' he promised solemnly, 'we'll return on our anniversary. We'll have to,' he added, 'to pay our respects to the goddess of Moon Cove.'

He took her by the hand and they began to walk back across the sands. Already the sun was beginning to set, shadows purpling beneath the palms and the vast sky a hymn of gold.

Judy had taken her beloved Tine to the secret place where she had kept her record of the memories that had meant so much to her in those days when she had almost despaired of being rescued. Together they read them, sitting side by side on the beach while the baby played in the shallows that lapped around their feet. He read how she had loved him then in secret, how she had longed to hold him in her arms. When he had finished, he put his arms round her and cradled her for a long time.

When at last he spoke he said, 'This is the story of my love too, but I had no way of expressing it other than to keep you safe from harm.' He tapped the sheaf of brittle leaves whereon their love was written. 'This is only the first part of our story,' he told her. 'The best is yet to come.'

As the day drew to a close and the sound of the returning helicopter broke the soporific whispers of the breaking waves, they took one last look at the place that would always hold such special memories for them.

'Goodbye,' said Judi with a sigh of contentment. 'We shall be back ... we shall be back ...'

Next month's Romances

Each month, you can choose from a world of variety in romance with Mills & Boon. These are the new titles to look out for next month.

THE GOLDEN MASK ROBYN DONALD

THE PERFECT SOLUTION CATHERINE GEORGE

A DATE WITH DESTINY MIRANDA LEE

THE JILTED BRIDEGROOM CAROLE MORTIMER

SPIRIT OF LOVE EMMA GOLDRICK

LEFT IN TRUST KAY THORPE

UNCHAIN MY HEART STEPHANIE HOWARD

RELUCTANT HOSTAGE MARGARET MAYO

TWO-TIMING LOVE KATE PROCTOR

NATURALLY LOVING CATHERINE SPENCER

THE DEVIL YOU KNOW HELEN BROOKS

WHISPERING VINES ELIZABETH DUKE

DENIAL OF LOVE SHIRLEY KEMP

PASSING STRANGERS MARGARET CALLAGHAN

TAME A PROUD HEART JENETH MURREY

STARSIGN

GEMINI GIRL LIZA GOODMAN

Available from Boots, Martins, John Menzies, W.H. Smith, most supermarkets and other paperback stockists.

Also available from Mills & Boon Reader Service, P.O. Box 236, Thornton Road, Croydon, Surrey CR9 3RU.